Around the World in Eight Days

AROUND THE WORLD IN EIGHT DAYS

Ron Kovic

City Lights Books
San Francisco

Library of Congress Cataloging in Publication Data

Kovic, Ron
  Around the world in eight days.
  I. Title
PS3561.O86A88   1984   813'.54   84-19897
ISBN 0-87286-161-9
ISBN 0-87286-162-7 (pbk.)

Cover: Painting by Ron Kovic
       Photograph by Jeffrey Blankfort

CITY LIGHTS BOOKS are edited by Lawrence Ferlinghetti and Nancy J. Peters and published at the City Lights Bookstore, 261 Columbus Avenue, San Francisco, California 94133.

For Pat

Now you may think this story is crazy, but it really happened. I did go around the world in eight days without the use of any jet planes, or any other aircraft including balloons or anything else like that.

I had made a bet with my former Cub Scout troop leader, a guy named Bobby Thompson who, by the way, had been recently released from state prison for a crime I won't go into right now, other than it had to do with a small child, a couple of animals, and a rainbow. Anyway, this guy Bobby Thompson and I made a bet this one afternoon, while sitting on his dad's porch, which is right across the street from the Parkside Junior High School field, where I used to play when I was a kid growing up in Massapequa. Bobby was acting really angry and bitter that day because it had only been a while since he had gotten out of prison, and he still had this bad attitude problem, the way everybody just released from prison has. He was just cursing and spitting on the living room rug of his mom's place, talking to me all about the way jail was, and all the people he had met, and all the things he had learned there.

I was amazed, because this guy, when I was growing up, was probably one of the most respected guys you'd ever want to know from the town. He was like some kind of Big Guy Hero to us when we were kids, and I remember how shocked and absolutely saddened I was when I found out he had been sent away to prison. Bobby Thompson! God—could that be the same guy who was our Scout leader? I found it hard to believe that the guy I most looked up to had gone away to prison and done all those things they said he did.

After a while we went out on Bobby's front stoop and just sat there for a while, Bobby and me just looking out at the beautiful field across from his house and saying nothing for a long time. Bobby kept cursing all the things that had happened to him in his life. And all of a sudden that's when I told him I could go around the world in eight days.

"Well, sure you can, anybody can these days," he told me, wiping his mouth with his sleeve. "What's so big a deal about that?" he continued.

I then explained to Bobby that I meant around the world in eight days without the use of any jets or airplanes.

"Without no airplanes?" shouted Bobby, now standing up on his dad's stoop, seeming all of sudden to come alive. "No planes?" he said again.

"That's right," I told him. "I know I can circle the globe in eight days. I'll bet you I can," I said in almost a whisper, still looking out at the field we played on as kids.

Bobby sat back down on the stoop and, after leaning his head back, almost looking directly up at the sky, he spit, with everything in him sending the wet mass arching out into the gravel street. "How much you wanna bet white man?" he shouted.

"I'll bet everything I own, and everything in my savings account," I said, meaning every word of it.

"OK," you're on, eight days around the world from start to finish. It's a bet," shouted Bobby.

At this moment Bobby's father walked out, having overheard our conversation, and immediately bet his life savings that I couldn't make it around the world at all. "You'll get killed by the Indians before you ever reach Tucson," he said, slapping me on my back.

But I didn't let Bobby and his father bother me. I just shook their hands and, after asking them what month of the year it was, tore off down the street in my new tennis sneakers, made a left on Broadway and ran as hard as I could through my town. There was the A&J Sporting Goods store on my right, with the Massapequa jackets hanging in the window next to the white wool athletic socks. And then I went under the train trestle where the Long Island Railroad trains run. I could see the Massapequa diner over the other side of the Sunrise Highway and I made a right on Sunrise and headed west, sprinting so hard I felt my lungs were going to bust. I didn't know what Bobby Thompson and his father were doing, but I was trying to get around the world in eight days without any airplanes and I was determined to do it. By that afternoon I had passed New York City and had gotten as far as the New Jersey Turnpike. I knew some people in Cincinnati and I hoped that if I kept running and sticking out my thumb along the highway somebody would pick me up and give me a ride through Pennsylvania and into Ohio.

I was in luck. A guy in a truck stopped and took me all the way to Pittsburgh. I thanked him and then almost immediately got a ride from a short little fat guy who couldn't stop talking all the way into the outskirts of Cincinnati. I had been going almost seventeen hours now and I was tired and really hungry and the little fat guy was kind enough to buy me some hot soup and a sandwich at a Howard Johnson's. After I ate I felt good and spent a lot of time staring at all the cute girls in their tight skirts who would come into the place with their boyfriends who always had such serious looks on their faces. A couple of times I was lucky enough to look right up one cute girl's skirt and I think I saw her underpants once. She closed her legs together when she realized I was staring up her skirt and I turned my head away embarrassed that she had caught me.

I daydreamed most of the afternoon away not even realizing that the guy who had picked me up had left. He was such a nice guy for picking me up, I thought to myself, then I got up and ran out the door and started running down the street remembering I had to make it around the world in eight days. It was getting dark and I had made it all the way to Cincinnati. I'm doing great, I thought to myself. Within a few minutes I was at Eden Street where I stayed the night with a bunch of people I had known from a couple of years before. Everybody was excited and really impressed when I told them I was trying to make it around the world in eight days and I had bet this guy and his father I could do it.

"Everything you own?" they asked, almost as if to question my sanity.

"Yes," I told them, "everything I own, and I'm going to make it too."

They all seemed very proud of me and one of the girls even offered to let me sleep with her that night, and I did. We made out and cuddled most of the night to the soft soothing sounds on her stereo. I think Aaron Copeland's "Appalachian Spring" was playing and I thought of my childhood and cried.

The next morning I was up at the crack of dawn kissing Beverly goodbye. I ran downstairs, gobbled up an orange out of the refrigerator. Eating it peel and all, I raced out of the house and in the morning light ran with everything I had in me toward the main highway. By nine o'clock I had gotten there and after a couple unsuccessful attempts to get a ride, I started running along the highway. I headed north toward the Ohio Turnpike and thought of my father for a moment and all the trips we took to Wisconsin in his station wagon when we were kids. It was only an hour or so away and I knew that when I got there I'd start heading west out toward Chicago where my friend Loretta the cab driver lived. I loved Loretta. She had been a friend of mine for years and I knew that if I could just get to Chicago I would meet with Loretta and let her know what I was doing. Maybe she'd even want to come with me, I thought. No, I thought again, that's crazy, she won't want to go. She's probably busy the way she always is, driving her cab or working on a movie or something. It was a long and difficult morning, but by early that afternoon, and after a couple of wild and really crazy rides, to say the least, I had made it to just outside the little town of Cicero, Illinois, where I was let off by a kind woman who had told me she was a grade school teacher.

I talked with a few people at the bus station for a while, one guy really drunk and trying to get back to Chattanooga for the funeral of his father, and a short, fast-talking pretty woman in pigtails whom I almost fell in love with at first sight because of the way she immediately grabbed me with her eyes, and her hillbilly dress that made her seem more like a guy than a girl. I left both of them and ran down the street where I stopped to rest next to a post office at a cafe which also had a pool table in it and two pretty waitresses who smiled at me, and whose eyes sparkled when I walked in.

"A ham and egg on rye," I shouted before I had even sat down.

"Ham and egg on rye," repeated the one waitress, "coming right up."

I sat there eating and scribbling on one of the napkins on the table with my pen, doodling and drawing little pictures of naked women and men in the sex act. Some of the men I drew had surprised expressions on their faces as they look down at their enormous penises, and I drew one man's hand and arm, making it a big penis. It was at that moment one of the waitresses bent over, spotted what I had drawn and began to scream.

Maybe Cicero, Illinois isn't the best place to be

14

drawing penises attached to the ends of men's hands—this was my first thought as I quickly turned the napkin over. Crumpling it up, I tossed it on top of my mashed potato which had come with the ham and egg on rye and which I hadn't eaten because I don't eat carbohydrates so I can keep my waist thin and look attractive and sexy to the women.

"Don't get excited. I can explain, please," I shouted to the waitress. "I'm an artist. I'm from New York," I said, "and what I was drawing was just something from a dream I had once about my hand turning into a penis."

The woman kept screaming though, and now everyone in the place was looking over at us. "Please," I said, whispering now, "it was just a dream I had. I was working my dream out on paper. I wasn't being dirty. I wasn't drawing dirty things. Look, you see my hand?" I said, wiggling my fingers. "It's not a penis. It's nothing like a penis, but in the dream it turned into a penis. You could call it a deformity, an amputation. It was a freak thing, you know," I said, trying to grab her arm, "but it didn't bother me. I felt comfortable with my hand turning into a penis. It fit. Can you understand? It fit and that's why I was drawing it on that napkin because it was all right. It was art, my dreams, I had nothing to be ashamed of."

The police took me away at four that afternoon, handcuffing my wrists behind my back and taking the crumpled-up napkin I had tossed on top of the mashed potatoes for evidence. By now it was all soaked in gravy and I was scared. What a stupid place to draw penises was my only thought, I'll never draw

15

a penis in Cicero, Illinois again. The cops put me in the paddy wagon and took me away. At the jail a few minutes later I was read my rights and deposited in a small holding cell where I sat almost two hours.

"What am I charged with? What are the charges?" I shouted, but no one would answer me.

About fifteen minutes later a cop, immaculately dressed in his uniform, walked up to me and told me I had been charged with having a dirty mind. "That's right," said the cop without blinking. "You're charged with having filthy thoughts and for putting those filthy thoughts down on paper within the presence of a minor." It seemed like a really serious charge and the cop told me I could get up to thirty or forty years for what I had done if I didn't come up with some kind of alibi, and soon.

I didn't know what to do so I started dancing in my cell and singing this song about you lost that loving feeling by the Righteous Brothers. "Baby, baby I get down on my knees for you," I sang. "But don't don't don't don't take my love away ... Baby Baby Baby Baby I need your love! I need your love. You lost that loving feeling oh ooh that loving feeling!"

And after a while and a couple of loud choruses of the song, one of the cops—a young guy—walked up to my cell. He must have really loved the song because he had tears in his eyes and this really beautiful look on his face.

"That was really nice," he told me. "I really love that song."

I was amazed that the cop liked my song so much, and to my surprise he asked me to do a few more. I obliged him singing "Up on the Roof" by the Drifters which he really loved and followed it with "Runaway" by Del Shannon and the song "Hats Off to Larry" which both of us sang together like old high school buddies. By the time I sang "Runaway" the second time, quite a few of the guy's buddies had walked over to my cell and had joined in. It's like a barbershop quartet, I thought to myself. I couldn't believe how well we all harmonized together and it was all happening in jail too. Unbelievable, I thought, this is amazing. After a couple of repeats of the songs I had already sung, I went into a rendition of the old Sixties classic "Under the Boardwalk" and then sang the old Elvis favorite—"You Ain't Nothin' But A Hound Dog." I thought of Ed Sullivan for a moment and was amazed at how one of the cops so closely resembled the famous TV host.

"You look just like Ed Sullivan," I said to the cop, who blushed and turned his head away shyly, still trying to sing: "Under the boardwalk, out of the sun ... under the boardwalk we'll be havin' some fun."

It went on and on like that, a real party for almost three hours, with some of the cops pulling their guns and handcuffs out of the backs of their belts and beating them, clinking and clanking them against the bars of my jail cell to the wonderful beat of the great golden oldies we were singing. It seemed by the looks on their faces they hadn't had this much fun in years. When we finished it was almost six o'clock and time for the new shift to come on. All the cops reached into the cell to shake my hand and thanked me for making them feel so happy.

17

"You don't know what you did for me," said one cop, squeezing my hand as hard as he could, not being able to let go. "You brought back feelings I haven't felt in years."

I couldn't believe how nice the cops were to me and it seemed they had even forgotten the pictures I had drawn on the napkin. Maybe they'll let me go, I thought, but when the new shift came on they weren't friendly at all. They were all business after reading my report. One of the new cops who had just come on duty walked up to my cell and called me a pervert.

I was worried now. I couldn't afford to lose time like this, but it looked like there wasn't much I could do. My only response was to start dancing and singing again. I sang the song "The Battle of New Orleans." "Well, we ran through the briars and we ran through the brambles, we ran through the bushes where a rabbit couldn't go; we ran so fast the hounds couldn't catch us, down the Mississippi to the Gulf of Mexico."

The cop told me he found me very entertaining, then told me he was going to let me make one phone call because that was the law. I thanked him and, when I got to the phone which was down a long depressing green corridor, decided to call my friend Loretta, in Chicago, collect.

"Hello Laurie," I said. "I'm in jail in Cicero, Illinois. That's right. I got busted down here. Would you please help me, Laurie?"

She said she'd be right down in her cab.

"Thanks, Laurie," I said, hanging up the phone. The tall cop led me back to the cell and after talking with me for a while in a very friendly manner slammed the cell door shut. I waited for Laurie who was always great in tough situations such as these, and dreamed of making it to Chicago late that night if I was lucky, with plans of continuing my journey the following morning. I was well into the second day of my trip and even though things looked pretty tough, I still had no doubt I would be able to make it around the world in the eight days allotted me in my bet with Bobby Thompson and his father.

By nine o'clock that night, Loretta had arrived and immediately tried to convince the cops in that amazing persuasive manner of hers that actually they had arrested the wrong man—and that the real pervert was a guy two inches shorter than me who had escaped on a bus to South America hours before.

"You've got the wrong guy," she told them. "I hate to mess up your day but this guy you've got in the cell is a dear friend of mine who never had a dirty thought in his life. In fact," said Laurie, "he wanted to be a priest when he was seventeen and as far as I know he's still a virgin."

"Still a virgin?" said one of the cops, seeming very surprised.

"That's right," said Loretta almost in a whisper. "He never got it on in his life."

"Well then, what's all this stuff about him drawing a penis at the end of this guy's hand?" said the cop showing Laurie the gravy-stained napkin. "The evidence is right here."

"It was just a dream," said Loretta, trying not to seem startled by the picture. "We all dream. You do, I do," said Loretta. "Everybody dreams things, but that

19

doesn't make it a crime. Since when have dreams become accountable to the law? Since when have dreams become crimes?" asked Loretta. "My uncle Eddie never convicted anyone of dreaming."

"What the hell's your uncle Eddie got to do with anything?" asked the cop.

"Uncle Eddie? You never heard of my Uncle Eddie? Eddie Dimaggio?" said Loretta.

"Sure I heard of him. Everybody's heard of Judge Dimaggio. He's some kind of legend in Chicago, isn't he?" said the cop.

"That's right," said Loretta. "He's one of the most important judges in Cook County."

"Holy shit. Judge Dimaggio," said the cop again.

"Or Eddie D., as his friends like to call him," said Loretta interrupting.

"Yeah, yeah, I know who you mean," said the cop. "I'm well aware of who Judge Dimaggio is."

"Well, I just want you to know," said Loretta, "he's personal friends with the guy you got in that cell."

"Jesus Christ," said the cop. "Why didn't you tell us you was relatives with Judge Dimaggio."

"You shoulda told us in the first place," said his partner now trying to sound polite.

"We're sorry," said the cop. "You're right, we should never have arrested him. We made a big mistake," said his partner.

"You did," said Loretta. "You arrested the wrong man."

Laurie and I raced back toward Chicago in her car. I felt so happy to get out of Cicero and promised myself I'd never go back to that town ever again.

20

"Thanks, Laurie," I said. "Thanks so much for helping me get out of jail."

"Don't mention it," said Laurie. She stepped on the gas.

I told Laurie all about my bet and how I was trying to get around the world. "And I know I can do it in time," I shouted.

It was well past midnight when we got into Chicago, and Loretta took me to one of her favorite bars, a place called O'Rourke's where all the writers and journalists hang out. It was really an interesting place and I was just so happy to get out of Cicero I didn't care where I was. I had a couple drinks—diet soda because I'm not into alcohol—and told Loretta all about my trip and how amazing it had been so far. She was a wonderful listener the way she always is and I went on for almost forty-five minutes in the crowded bar, telling all about the bet I had made with Bobby Thompson and his father and how I absolutely expected to make it around the world in only eight days.

"That's amazing," said Laurie above the loud voices in the bar. "You really think you can make it?"

"Sure," I told her. "I don't see why not."

After an hour or so we left the bar. Walking through the wonderful late night streets of Chicago I remembered all the times in my life that I had come to the city. There was Wrigley Field and the Cubs and the times Loretta and I would go to the games and sit in the bleachers in back of the fabulous park that was probably the most beautiful old baseball park in America. They still didn't have night games at the park. They had never installed lights in the old classic place and probably never would. There was Ray's Bleacher Bum Bar we'd go to every time after the games to drown our woes and sorrows for the poor hapless Cubbies in song and nonstop dancing with the wonderful Chicagoans who were the most loyal fans in the country. There was Melvin's Cafe on Rush Street and a wonderful folk song place called Somebody Else's Troubles and a half dozen more fantastic places and amazing and interesting people Loretta had introduced me to over the years.

When we got to Loretta's place over on Halsted Street we ran up the sixty or so steps. Loretta gave me some blankets and covers and a little room I always used whenever I was in town. I slept well that night and awoke early, eager to continue my journey. I knew all too well that my time was getting very short. This would be the third day of my adventure. I'd have to leave Chicago immediately and, by means I had neither figured out nor decided yet, head deep into Iowa and Kansas and maybe the Rocky Mountains by the following day. I was hopeful, extremely hopeful and my body pulsated with a new and tremendously determined energy and hope. I was on my way. I said goodbye to Loretta, running for a moment into her room to tell her that I was leaving and I'd call her as soon as I got to Tucson. I ran down the steps of her place almost tripping and falling on my face from excitement.

"Woooo weeee!" I screamed as I got to the sidewalk, startling a couple of people who were walking by. I started running like a madman straight down Halsted Street dodging in and out of the frantic morning traffic. By nine-thirty that morning I had caught my first ride from an affable little fellow who was heading to the airport—of all places—to pick up his aunt, a woman named Nan who, the guy claimed, was coming in from Baltimore for a visit with the family.

"That sounds really nice," I said, trying to make conversation with my first ride of the day and happy that I was just moving and heading anywhere. The guy stepped on the gas pedal of his little car and soon we were roaring through traffic.

"Where ya headed?" asked the guy.

"Across the country," I said confidently.

"Flying out?" he asked.

"Oh, no. I'm not allowed to fly," I told him. "I made a bet with this guy in New York and I can't use any airplanes."

"You can't what?" said the guy taking his cap off, scratching his head and looking at me like I was a little crazy.

"I'm not allowed to fly. It's part of the bet."

The guy didn't say anything and soon we were at the airport, and he let me out and I thanked him profusely, shaking his hand and wishing him luck with his aunt and everything else in his life.

I sat at the airport for a while, not the least bit tempted to buy a ticket and fly the rest of the way around the world, cheating Bobby Thompson and his father out of their life savings. I was certain things would work out my way, and I was right because before long some guy in a big flatbed truck stopped and asked me if I needed a lift deep into Kansas.

23

"Sure do!" I said as I jumped into the huge front seat cab. "I'm going as far as you're going."

We tore off leaving Chicago far behind, out into the beautiful midwest countryside. The guy—a tall guy who looked exactly like Abraham Lincoln—told me he was a shoe salesman who had stolen the truck he was now driving the night before.

"Are you kidding me?" I said, feeling both scared and excited at the same time.

"Yeah," said the guy, who told me his name was Pete but his friends called him Butch. I turned the dial on his radio and the song "The Boy from New York City" was playing.

"Oh, I love that," said Butch, leaning over and turning up the song full blast. "Oowee you ought to come and see—the boy from New York City." We started beating the dashboard of the cab singing together at the top of our lungs as we barrelled through the last bits of Illinois. "He's the most from coast to coast . . . Oh yeah talkin' about the boy, the boy from New York City—he's fair—oooo that boy can dance—talkin' about the boy."

We crossed the Iowa-Illinois line just as the song ended. The speedometer read ninety-five and I remembered I hadn't felt happier than at that moment in my entire life. This guy was amazing whether he stole that truck or not. Butch switched the dial around on the radio and found this great blues song that made us both feel so sad and teary-eyed.

"God, that's beautiful," I said as we slowed down for a pay toll that was just ahead. Butch was working the gearshift like a champ, fingering its spectacular little diamond-shaped ball like a real master. I loved watching him work the stick and the clutch and at the same time have the complete composure to roll down his window, lean out at a forty-five-degree angle with a big smile on his face, wish the guy in the toll booth a nice day and drop four quarters into his hand.

We roared off once again and within a couple of minutes Butch had the old flatbed up around a hundred miles an hour, the radio turned up full blast and both of us were acting like a couple of teenagers on a wild weekend romp through the countryside.

"At this rate," I screamed above the noise, "We'll be in Peking by morning!"

"Peking?" said Butch, his happy face suddenly turning into an angry frown. "I'm only going as far as Kansas."

"Well then, we'll be in Kansas by the morning," I said. I figured I'd better humor Butch whose sudden and unexplained mood swing, I must admit, had completely baffled me and left me even more confused about the man than when our trip had begun earlier that day. Butch then shut the radio off and, for reasons to this day I cannot understand, we rode in total silence through most of the state of Iowa, Butch not so much as even glancing over at me.

What had begun as one of the happiest days of my entire life had now become a living hell so to speak that made no sense to me at all. I fidgeted around in my seat trying to keep from going crazy and slept for a while, wondering what the hell it was I said to Butch that had made him so upset. After a while I decided whatever it was I'd probably never know, and Butch was probably a very upset and confused person to begin with. And why was I getting so uptight about the whole thing—this guy who looked like Abraham Lincoln not wanting to talk with me just because I said the word Peking. I had a free ride to Kansas nonstop all the way, both of us together there in the cab, one hundred miles an hour, the goddamn gas pedal pushed to the floor, no music, no talking. Who the hell cared, I thought. I was trying to get around the world, and if this guy was going to help me part of the way who cared if he talks to me or not.

"Yeah," I suddenly shouted, moving closer to Butch, pushing myself almost on top of him. "Who the fuck cares if you talk to me or not—or if you stole this truck. And you've got to wear a hearing aid because you're deaf. Isn't that true Butch? You're a deaf mute aren't you?" I said, poking him in the ribs. "You can't hear a goddamn thing can you?" I taunted, trying to break his silence. "This is maddening, maddening!" I shouted. "Don't you know what you're doing to me?"

Just at that moment Butch let go of the steering wheel, grabbed his head and started screaming at the top of his lungs. The truck swerved sharply and violently to the left, jacknifed wickedly and landed in a ditch, knocking me completely unconscious for what seemed hours, though I was later to be told by the highway patrolman and a young kid from the ambulance crew that I had been trapped in the cab only minutes when the fire began. If it hadn't been for a couple of passing motorists and two Cub Scouts who flagged down the patrol car, both Butch and I would surely have burned alive in the wreck.

Butch was taken away to a local hospital and I, though still dazed and bleeding profusely through my mouth and lip, refused medical treatment and insisted on continuing my journey, positioning myself back on the highway. I stuck out my thumb and cried out for someone to stop and pick me up.

"Help me! Help me!" I shouted. The highway patrolman who probably thought I was a little touched, to say the least, by my accident offered to take me as far as the next town, where he said I could wash up and see a doctor who was, he said, a friend of his, if I needed to. We rode back to town and I could see the cop really admired me for my courage and the way I had been so tough and refused any medical treatment.

"You've got a lot of guts," he said softly as we raced down the highway at what seemed like an incredible speed.

"Thanks," I told him with a deep sigh, which only now began to uncover the absolute and total fear I must have really felt over the whole agonizing mess. I began to cry.

"It's OK," said the cop. "We're all human. Even your buddy who caused that accident."

"Caused it?" I asked. "That's right," said the cop. "Butch Henderson. He's been causing crackups and accidents out here for years."

"What?" I said, not believing what I had just heard.

"That's right," he said. "A seven-car head-on collision with a trailer truck last March, two jackknifes into that same ditch four years ago. He went over a bridge just north of here in a little VW and there was nothing left but him. Each time in a different car he steals from the city," said the cop shaking his head.

"I can't believe that."

"It's true," said the cop. "This guy is a certified maniac. He's been stealing and wrecking cars for years."

"How come he never got killed?" I asked.

"I guess he's just been lucky," said the patrolman. "He killed fourteen people in the last twenty-one years, including both his sons, his wife and his seventy-six-year-old grandmother. He's such a nice guy," said the cop, scratching his head. "Everybody loves Butch, until you get in his car and go down the road a ways, then he starts acting crazy."

"He did it with me," I said grabbing the cop's sleeve.

"Right," said the cop. "He sucks you in, then whammo! He goes berserk. You better be careful," said the cop, letting off a little on the accelerator with his foot as we eased into town. "There's a lot of crazy people out there. Where you goin' anyway?"

"I'm going around the world in eight days," I told him matter-of-factly.

"Oh," said the cop, pausing for a moment. "Then you better be extra careful, you don't know what kind of nuts you're going to find out there," he said, pointing his hand out west beyond the town.

When I insisted again I didn't need any medical treatment and I could make it on my own ok, he let me off at the bus depot. The name of the town was Miranda and it reminded me of a famous court decision I had read about when I was studying political science at Hofstra University out on Long Island in 1970. For a moment I thought of my Poli Sci class and the cute girls I used to stare at all the time, hoping I could find someone to love me. The bus station was almost completely empty except for an old man who was sleeping soundly on a wooden bench by the Coke machine and a pretty young woman with long flowing dark hair that was beautifully braided with a long thin red ribbon tied delicately in a bow at the back.

"Excuse me," I said to the woman, not the least bit intimidated by her beauty. "Do you know when the next bus is leaving west? I'm trying to get to Kansas by tomorrow morning, and it's very important I get there as soon as I can."

The woman, who now turned, facing me, looked even more beautiful than I had first imagined from afar. She spoke slowly at first in very measured succinct tones, explaining to me that she was an exchange student from Brazil and spoke very little English. "I speak little English," she said with a dainty little smile which honest to God melted my heart, and I must admit made me want to quit the trip right then and there on the spot to find out who this lovely delightful woman was and where she was going. Maybe if I was lucky I could go with her.

"I am going to Kansas too," she said in her cute little accent.

"How are you getting there?" I asked.

"By bus," said the woman, now looking concerned and somewhat startled as she spotted my bloody lip from the accident.

"Señor," she shouted, suddenly waking up the old man who had been sleeping on the bench, "you are wounded."

"No, no, señorita," I said, trying the little Spanish I knew. "Señor esta bien. I'm OK. I'm OK. It's really nothing. I got hurt in a car crash," I explained. "You see?" I said, opening my mouth to show her the gaping wound just under my tongue. "I'll heal, really. It's no big deal. I'm alive aren't I?" I said, sticking my thumb in my ear, waving it back and forth and trying to make her laugh. "Do do do do do do do," I sang in a silly voice as I tapdanced before her on the tips of my toes.

Within moments the pretty little señorita had produced a tissue from her purse and was dabbing my lip and mouth carefully trying to stop the flow of blood that still trickled slowly like rain drops down my neck and onto my spring jacket.

"Oh, you don't have to do that."

A couple of minutes later I found out from one of the guys that worked at the bus station ticket-counter that a Greyhound would be coming into the station and leaving almost instantaneously for Kansas City and that it would arrive there about seven o'clock the next day.

"That's perfect," I told him. "That's just what I want." The woman from Brazil also bought a ticket and although we couldn't communicate that well because of the language difference, I told her I'd be happy if she sat with me on the trip to Kansas City. She agreed and told me her name was Carmen. The bus came in exactly when it was supposed to arrive and both Carmen and I got aboard and went way to the back where we found a nice seat. Before we even got a chance to get comfortable the sleek Greyhound tore off almost instantaneously just as the guy at the ticket counter had told me it would. Looking toward the front of the bus I saw that a number of interesting people had gotten on the bus too.

Immediately I put my arm around Carmen, drawing her toward me. "Señorita es muy bonita." I said softly as I leaned over and nibbled a bit on her ear. We roared out of town.

The bus driver, a little guy with a baseball cap on his head who was wearing the most defiant and determined look on his face seemed obssessed with getting us to our destination as quickly as possible.

"This is great," I told Carmen. "I'm so glad I met you and I'm really glad you don't mind me hugging you and kissing you."

"Oh, I do not mind," said Carmen, blushing, "but please . . . " She didn't finish what she was saying, but I understood she needed her own space and privacy and probably was the type of girl who liked to get involved with a man slowly.

"OK, OK, I get the message," I said, sticking both of my hands up in the air directly over my head. I'll be cool, don't worry, it's gonna be all right."

For a moment I just sat there with my hands folded in my lap, staring out the window as it grew darker and the night came on. I was approaching the end of the third day and I was still hundreds of miles from Kansas City and not quite half way across the country yet. I'll make it, I thought to myself. I know I will. Carmen had fallen asleep and I couldn't help but look once again at her beautiful and delicate face. Oh, God, she was beautiful. I looked down at her legs and for a moment thought of putting my hand on her kneecap, but at the last minute decided not to. Instead I sighed a deep somewhat frustrated sigh and closed my eyes and slept.

We rode all night and well into the next day and I dreamed of my father and he had a hammer and both of us in the dream were on the porch roof of my house in Massapequa and dad was hammering in nails and I was helping him. It was a good dream and when I awoke I felt lonely for a few minutes, thinking of my father who now lived in Florida and was too old to build houses any more.

The bus driver told us over the loudspeaker system that we'd be making four or five stops before we got into Kansas City and anybody who had to go to the bathroom should go now. The sun was tremendously hot when we pulled into the small town called North Platte and Carmen excused herself to go to the bathroom. I just smiled as she stepped over me, walking down the aisle and I closed my eyes for a second. I was exhausted and the whole trip, the whole crazy last three days seemed to be catching up with me.

I can't remember what happened next, only that an hour or so later I awoke suddenly. Carmen was gone. Where was she? I stood up and ran to the front of the bus, my heart beating almost out of control.

"What happened? What happened to my friend the South American woman?" I asked the bus driver.

"Get back in your seat!" he shouted coldly. "There's no talking with the driver allowed when the bus is in motion. Can't you read the sign?"

"But the girl I was with . . . the woman sitting next

to me. What happened? I fell asleep. She got off at the last stop. Did you see what happened?"

"Sit down," yelled the driver, "or do I have to stop this bus and throw you off."

"All right, all right," I shouted back to the driver as I retreated back to my seat. Everybody was looking at me now like I was crazy. "All right, all right." I sat back in my seat feeling more lonely than I had felt in years. I thought she was going to Kansas City. I thought she told me she was going to the same place I was going. What had happened to her? I was really worried about her. Why didn't she get back on the bus? I felt hurt and abandoned. I was alone again thirty-seven miles from Kansas City.

"Next stop Kansas City," shouted the driver. "All passengers must disembark ... Last stop Kansas City." I was now fully awake and excited that we had at least made it to Kansas City. The hell with Carmen, I thought to myself. Who was she anyway? What was that little South American woman up to? The hell with women! I was on the road in the middle of the greatest most interesting exciting adventure of my life and nobody, not even beautiful Carmen, was going to stop me from enjoying myself. And then for some unexplained reason, as we pulled into the Kansas City Greyhound bus station, I thought of Bobby Thompson and his father, probably still asleep in their house in Massapequa because neither Bobby nor his father worked and both loved to sleep in late every morning sometimes even until well past noon. I wonder if they're wondering where I am right now, I thought. Maybe they were even dreaming about me.

I got off the bus in Kansas City, stretching my tired legs, happy to be finally off the bus for a while. It was nine a.m. and the station was surprisingly crowded for this time of the morning, filled with all sorts of people who seemed in a fantastic hurry to get one place or another. I ran out of the bus depot as fast as I could, not really knowing where I was going. I just ran with everything there was in me past buildings and shops and schools and the early morning Kansas City traffic with its beeping horns and hurrying busy people going off to whatever they do in Kansas City. It was early afternoon when I got to the edge of Kansas City. Having run almost the entire width of the city I felt exhausted and exhilarated at the same time. I've got to get to Tuscon, I kept thinking to myself. Tuscon, Arizona, and I'll be almost across the country. I got to the main highway where I stuck out my thumb and began hitching, hoping I'd get a ride right away.

"Come on, come on!" I'd shout to people who would pass me in their cars. "I'm a nice guy. Come on, pick me up!" I'd shout, and that's exactly what this one guy did. He was a real quiet guy named Nick. He was tall and sunburned and he was wearing a big cowboy hat. I knew I was really in the West now and I was glad. Maybe now I'd begin to start to cover more ground. I needed to if I was going to make it. Nick very politely asked me how far I was going.

"Tucson," I said. "If I could get to Tucson that would be really great."

"Really?" said the guy. "That's where I'm headed. I live in Tucson."

"Fantastic," I told him, jumping in the front seat of

his car. We sped off down the highway. "Boy, am I lucky running into you."

"No problem." He stepped hard on the gas. "Mind if I drive a little fast?"

"No, not at all, go as fast as you want." The guy must have thought I meant it because a few minutes later he had his little Chevy up to almost a hundred miles an hour.

"Wow? You're really flying," I told him.

"Yeah. Wanna see it go faster," he said without the least bit of fear in his voice.

"Sure," I said, only feeling a little bit afraid. "Let her rip ... "

The guy now jammed the gas pedal to the floor for everything it was worth, pushing the Chevy to its maximum speed.

"Whew," I sighed. "That's really fucking fast." And we kept at that speed, carefully dodging in and out of trucks and cars for almost an hour. We were really making great time now.

"Incredible!" I congratulated him and rolled down my window and stuck my hand a little ways out, feeling the incredible speed. Yes, we were making record time and if it hadn't been for the blowout three hundred miles east of Tucson and the things that happened to us with the Indians there, we would have been right on schedule.

When the tire blew Nick had this crazy look on his face and I swear to God I thought for sure we were gonners. But somehow, with an incredible cool and composure I find hard to describe, he held on to the wheel as we swerved wildly on the desert highway.

35

"Christ!" I shouted, "That was fantastic."

When we finally stopped the car to survey the damage both of us were amazed at how we ever survived. The tire and most of the rim had completely disintegrated. There was nothing left but a half-bent axle, and me and Nick somehow still alive. For a few minutes we just sat there on the hood of his broken-down Chevy trying to figure out what we were going to do next. There wasn't another car in sight and the sun was hot as could be. It was at that exact moment the Indians attacked us on their motorcycles. They came from the hills just above where we blew the tire and they were riding 1946 Indian motorcycles. They had feathers in their headbands and tomahawks and bows and arrows and long spears which looked more like jousting poles. There was dust everywhere, a huge enormous cloud, and the sound of their angry war whoops and the roar of their bikes. There must have been sixty of them roaring out of the hills, dust flying everywhere. It came as a complete surprise to me. But Nick didn't seem surprised at all.

"I've got some guns in the back seat," he shouted as if he had expected the attack all along.

"Guns?" I shouted. "I don't like guns."

"Get the fucking guns," ordered Nick, pointing toward the back seat in a way that made me feel really scared.

"OK, OK," I said, opening the car door and grabbing the two loaded thirty-eights on the back seat. I handed one of the pistols to Nick as the sound of the wild war whoops and roar of the motorcycles grew louder and louder, as the enormous cloud of dust and confusion and angry Indians came closer.

"Just fire into that cloud of dust," screamed Nick who, after positioning himself around the back part of the car, began firing. "Come on, come on," he screamed but I could not fire my pistol.

"You better start shooting that thing you fucking coward," said Nick, angrily pointing his smoking pistol directly at me, "or I'm going to start firing at you."

I knew immediately that Nick meant business and, against my better judgment, moral and religious beliefs, aimed a few inches above the cloud of noise and dust and began to fire again and again hoping with everything that was in me I'd miss the Indians on their motorcycles. I didn't have anything against them. In fact, I had a tremendous amount of respect for how they'd survived considering how cruel and criminal the white man had been to them during the Manifest Destiny period of our country's history.

"Stop thinking those fucking thoughts," threatened Nick, who by now, I was certain, had some kind of uncanny, intuitive or psychic ability to read people's minds.

"I'm sorry," I said, firing what was left in my pistol in the general direction of the angry mob of Indians advancing towards us. It was exactly at this moment that Nick took a bullet through his throat, choked, gurgled a bit on his own blood and died. At first, I honest to God admit I felt relief. Who was this guy anyway to try and tell me to pick up a gun and kill people I had nothing against. I had nothing against these Indians, like I said before, and I didn't care what Nick told me to do. I threw my gun down into the sand and lay flat on my stomach with my face pressed up against the rear tire of Nick's little Chevy hoping and praying nobody would hurt me. The cloud of dust now surrounded me, the noise was deafening. I saw a spear fly right in front of my nose. There was banging on the hood of Nick's car, then suddenly I saw Nick, or at least it looked like Nick, being dragged and then carried above the shoulders of the Indians who were still on their motorcycles, with his scalp missing. I was frightened to death and for some reason at that moment when everything seemed lost, I bit squarely into the back tire with my teeth, gnawing on it like a mad dog until it exploded, the blast knocking me unconscious. I saw stars and when I awoke moments later the dust had settled and, above me, straddling his motorbike like a classic and rare Remington painting was the chief of the tribe with bones strapped to his chest and brightly-colored war paint, lovely colored feathers and long braided hair black and thick as night. And he was smiling, yes, smiling down at me.

"You need a ride to Frisco?" he said in a sort of Western drawl.

"Yeah, I sure do," I told him, getting up and shaking the dust from my pants. My two front teeth had been knocked loose from the force of the blast of the tire and I now spoke with somewhat of a lisp, but almost as if I were in a trance. I staggered toward him and, without questioning a thing, swung my leg over the back seat of his bike.

"Hold on tight," he said, and I did, squeezing him tightly around the waist. "My name is Takapusha, but you can call me Chief."

"San Francisco here we come," screamed the Chief. We roared off into the Arizona night, the Chief and me. And not far behind us was the wreck of the Chevy with two blown-out tires, a spear through the dashboard, and Nick with his head shaved off.

All through the night we rode, passing Tucson just before dawn and into the fifth day we raced, with me holding tightly to the Chief up through the mighty Sierras. We sped past Tahoe at three that afternoon and then roared through Reno just in time for the seven o'clock news. The Chief told me he was a news junky and never missed the national news. At exactly seven-thirty we were off again racing toward Sacramento, then down toward San Francisco. The air smelled great and the Chief, the expert bike rider he was, swerved seventeen times narrowly missing young deer that were trying to cross the road.

"Great going, wonderful, fantastic," I shouted, wondering if the Chief could even hear what I had said. "Unbelievable! Fantastic! Incredible!" I yelled, pounding the Chief on his back again and again.

"I heard what you just said, I heard every word of it," he said, leaning his head back towards me, "I concur. And besides, I love you," said the Chief as we roared over the most incredible mountain highway I've ever seen in my life. There were deep forests all around, great gorges that dropped suddenly almost out of sight twisting through time, and underground blasting with little bridges made of wood and straw.

"Chief, look at that!" I pointed down the great cliff, almost throwing us both off the bike. "Incredible, unbelievable," I kept repeating. "The forest, the woods, look at all the trees, Chief, look at it all, every-thing, it's unbelievable, oh, it's so beautiful, wow, man, boy oh boy, Chief, I've never seen anything like this in my life, the forest, the forest so thick and deep, incredibly deep, forests all around and pine cones as big as your headdress, Chief." Yes, everywhere and the smell and wonderful green and thickness that blocked out almost the entire sky. I could see small patches of blue and wonderful particles floating effortlessly of puffy white pajama-shaped clouds. I was dazed. I was staggered. Was the Chief coming on to me? I was cascading now. My mind seemed to flip over twiceways and it was at that moment I remem-bered LOVE was a four-letter word pasted up on Val-entine stationery. It was also a song Joan Baez sung once, and without further ado I gripped the Chief under the ceremonial bones strapped to his chest given to him by his girlfriend last Christmas and asked him if he wanted an artichoke while simultane-ously rubbing his big hairy chest with my hands.

"I hope this makes you feel better," I shouted, feel-ing almost ashamed, but not quite, and then confused by the gun he suddenly and violently pulled out of a holster strapped to the right side of his boot.

"Better be careful, White Man," he warned.

"I thought you needed a massage. I'm not gay. I'm straight, Chief," I yelled against the wind as loud as I could. "I thought you needed someone to touch you other than your mother and your angry girlfriend in Omaha."

"What I need is a cool breeze and a lake," said the Chief, jamming on the handlebar brakes of his 1946

Indian motorcycle. "I need a fishing pole, too," said the Chief as we pulled up to the side of the road, "and a half a quart of rum and some girls."

"Girls with yellow underpants and with lollypops in their mouths," I added.

"Yeah," said the Chief, jumping off his bike. "I want a chance to be somebody."

"We all do!" I agreed, slapping his back in a really friendly way.

"I want an end to human rights violations abroad," demanded the Chief.

"So do I," I agreed.

At that moment the Chief pulled out a match from a hotel he stayed in once in Minnesota and, after carefully unscrewing the gas tank of his bike and dabbing an old torn up t-shirt he had in his back pocket, he lit the bike on fire. Having somewhat figured what he was up to by the glint in his eye and books I've read, I jumped off the bike, did two back flips, a dozen cartwheels and two frog kicks as the bike exploded in a spectacular flash of molten flames.

"Woorsh, Bam, Wow, Zoom!" shouted the Chief as he began a wild dance around the flaming wreck, intermittently tearing off all his clothing, his beads, his beautiful colored beads and his photograph of Punch and Judy and his expired California driver's license, all of his feathers and two tickets to the policeman's ball in Omaha.

"You're naked," I said

"I'm free," said the Chief, now squatting in a beautiful clearing. He began to urinate carefully on a leaf. "You see that?" he asked. "You see the leaf?" He let out a deep sigh, "It reminds me of an angel."

The Chief's bike continued to burn out of control for well over an hour as I sat up against a great redwood tree and began to pray, saying dozens of Hail Marys.

"Hail Mary full of grapes the lord is swiss cheese," I yelled.

The Chief began to laugh wildly, still holding the piss-soaked leaf in his hand. Caressing it like a little baby, he began to yodel. "Bless it art thou amongst women," he sang.

"And blessit is the toot of they whom sneezes," I continued. I got up and ran over to him and threw my arm around his shoulder. "And our Father who art in heaven hollowed be thy brain."

"Yeah," said the Chief, his eyes now sparkling with anticipation.

"And deliver us a pizza," I sang. "Yeah, and deliver us a pizza from Shakeys Amen."

"Yeah, Amen," said the Chief, bowing his head sharply and running towards his bike that had suddenly and for unexplained reasons become as sparkling new as the day he had bought it the day after the war, in 1946.

Both the Chief and I made the sign of the cross, then jumped back on the bike, having both agreed that we had witnessed a miracle and that probably our lives would never be the same again. We tore off down the highway and it began to rain rosary beads and flypaper.

"Religion is like flypaper," announced the Chief, happy as hell to have his old Indian bike back.

"Not at all," I snapped back at him. "It's more like mentholatum deep heat rub."

"Yeah," growled the Chief. "It's like turkeys."

We raced into the night of the fourth day with me not even the least bit worried now about making it around the world in eight days. We roared all night down the incredible Sierras into Sacramento, then down the long and winding road toward San Francisco which I've always felt to be the most beautiful city in the world. The Chief had the old bike up to about a hundred and eleven miles an hour when we reached Berkeley and by the time we hit the Oakland Bay Bridge toll-gate I swore we were up to at least a hundred and twenty.

"Geronimo!" shouted the Chief as we roared past the toll plaza and raced across the Oakland Bay Bridge.

San Francisco was majestic, and I'll never forget how beautiful it looked that night all lit up like some kind of giant Christmas tree. There was Coit Tower which looked like a huge firehose nozzle sticking out of the ground, and half a dozen other spectacular buildings that stuck up toward the sky like a fortress. This was San Francisco, I thought to myself as the bike vibrated wildly and the Chief tried to slow it down a bit.

"Get off at the Broadway exit," I shouted still holding tightly to the Chief's waist.

Somehow the Chief was able to make the turn without throwing me off into the bay and within no time we were cruising into North Beach were I used to hang out all the time whenever I went to San Francisco.

"Stop at Enrico's," I told the Chief, and he did just

exactly as I asked him. "I know this guy Richard Daniels. He's really an unbelievable guy. He's been everywhere." I went on getting off the back of the bike. My legs felt weak and I wobbled up on to the sidewalk talking and talking with my hands and arms flying and jabbing every conceivable direction.

"You don't say," said the Chief, shutting off the engine of the bike.

"It's true," I told him "and if there's anyone who knows how I'm going to get the rest of the way around the world in the next three days it's Daniels," I said, shaking my head.

"Yeah," said the Chief, now climbing off his bike. "I think I heard of that guy."

Enrico's was still packed and buzzing with all the late night people that are there almost every night sitting and chatting in the wonderful outdoor cafe until two or three. On both sides of the street there were strip joints and while I went to make a phone call to try to get Richie, the Chief insisted on going to the belly dance place on the other side of the street where he said he knew one of the girls he said was named Kate. I told him I'd see him in a few minutes and ran into the back of Enrico's where the phone is, next to the men and women's bathrooms.

"Hey Rich, this is ... I just got into town. Yeah, yeah, Rich—I got this ride from an Indian in Tucson. Right, right. Yeah," I said, "it's a long story. I'll tell you when we get together. OK, OK," I said. "We'll be right over. See ya, Rich."

I went running back out of the cafe and spotted the Chief who seemed to be hassling with some cops on the other side of the street.

"Hey Chief," I shouted. "What's happening?"

"I'm OK," said the Chief, a bit wistful. After a few minutes and what appeared to be an intense conversation with the two policemen, he walked back across the street in a weird sort of bowlegged fashion that reminded me of an old Western movie.

"What was that all about?" I asked him.

"No big deal," said the Chief. "Seven years ago I was arrested for going on an emotional binge in the city of Cincinnati, Ohio. I got forty-one years for loitering and late alimony payments. I'm a crazy Indian," shouted the Chief as he bent down and did a perfect handstand in the middle of the street, stopping all the traffic in all directions. "Yokey Yokey," said the Chief. "Yokey Yokey," he sang again.

"Well, at least you're a good athlete," I said, trying to make the Chief feel better and it must have because he came out of the handstand in a perfect tuck and roll. "Beautiful," I said, applauding and then everybody at Enrico's started applauding too. The Chief blushed slightly, then began a dance on the sidewalk that lasted almost fifteen minutes before one of Enrico's bouncers, a guy from Thailand, tried to stop him from dancing without a permit. For a moment I thought the whole thing was going to turn into a barroom brawl, but the Chief cooled down and both of us jumped on the bike again and roared off to Richie's place.

"Shit," said the Chief sarcastically as we drove up and down the wonderful and incredible steep hills of San Francisco that always have a surprise waiting for you at the top that's magnificent and out of this world. The Chief then insisted on driving up the crookedest street in the world the wrong way and it was almost dawn and I said fuck it and we did it. We could have been killed but what did it matter anymore. I had crossed the Continent in a little less than five days.

The trip had been pretty remarkable so far, but it was going to take some doing to get me the rest of the way around the world in the few days I had left. And if anybody could, Richard Daniels—the famous war correspondent and world traveler—would help me out. He'd find a way for me to win the bet.

"Let's go to Richie's now," I urged the Chief who by now was falling asleep at the wheel because he was so incredibly tired and woozy from the whole crazy trip. "Just a little ways to go," I yelled, trying to encourage him. "Don't fall asleep now. We're almost to Richie's place," I told the Chief, slapping him on the back repeatedly, trying to keep him awake.

At one point, just as we got to about a mile or so from where Richie lived, the Chief blacked out completely and the bike kept going for almost a block and a half. The Chief slumped forward and collapsed on top of the handle bars, his huge nose pressed up against the horn.

We tore down Clement Street. Swerving wildly out of control I grabbed his waist as tightly as I could and threw him, like a sack of potatoes, to and fro—now trying to steer the bike myself.

Christ, I thought, he's got the throttle turned up full blast. The speedometer read one hundred and thirty and the engine sounded like a clown with a toothache. Up and down we went, careening off lamp posts and telephone poles, the Chief dead asleep at the wheel. And once again, as it suddenly seemed it was all over for the Chief and me, we smashed into a bakery shop just off Hyde Street, barrelled over two trucks parked illegally on Mission Street and jackknifed into a swimming pool where the bike sank to the bottom and I saved the Chief's life by grabbing him by his feathers and pulling him to safety.

"Are we there yet?" The Chief was choking and coughing.

"No, not yet," I said. I gave him mouth-to-mouth resuscitation by the side of the pool while somebody called the fire department. For some reason I began singing the Joan Baez song "Kumbaya my Lord, Kumbaya."

"Oh, Lord, Kumbaya," I crooned it softly to the Chief and held him tenderly in my arms, rocking him back and forth like a baby as the morning came. It was the sixth day of the trip and I was thirsty and aching all over. The Chief was comatose and though at first I thought of taking him to a hospital, I strapped him instead to my back and carried him straight up Montgomery Street along the trolley car tracks and began humming an old tune, the old Russian work song. "Yo ho heave ho, Yo ho heave ho, do do do de deddo you oh heave ho do do do do do do do do do do doe deo de do," I kept on singing.

At exactly seven-thirty that morning I arrived at Richard Daniels' place with the Chief still strapped tightly to my back.

"Richard! Richard!" I shouted, so happy to see my old friend again. Richard opened the door and we went in and collapsed on his rug.

"Hey, man—how's it going?" Richie was happy to see me, and he couldn't wait to help me find a way to get around the world in the next thee days.

"No problem," said Richie, walking into the room, spinning a globe around and around in his hand. "It's a big world." He sat down on the couch and grabbed a beer. He took a gigantic swig, as the world still spun around and around. "It's enormous," he said, propping his feet up on the Chief's head and putting both his hands behind his own head. My heart sank. I was beginning to think it would take a miracle. But Rich looked confident.

"And you've been everywhere, haven't you Rich." Richie just smiled.

"There isn't a man on the planet like you, Richie," I went on. "You've lived faster, gone further, and met more people and done more things than any member of your generation.

"He's amazing, he's incredible," I confided to the Chief who was now sleeping soundly on the floor.

Daniels was stupendous. There was no one like Daniels, no one would ever live like him, do the things he did. He wasn't afraid of anything. He just took off and went, and did whatever he wanted to when he wanted to. "It's my movie," he'd always say and he meant it. Born in a basement apartment on Market Street in San Francisco and raised by his grandmother, he'd grown up the hard way. By the time he was fourteen he had been arrested seven times, twice for car theft. He had knocked up nine girls by his senior year, and the day before he was to graduate from Lowell High School, he escaped San Francisco, hitching all the way across the country on seventy-two dollars. When he got down to Miami he caught a boat to Cuba just as the revolutionaries were marching into Havana. He always had a nose for news and an uncanny timing for historic events. He sensed when important things were going to happen and took off like a madman always making it there just in time. At an early age—though he couldn't spell to save his life—Richard Daniels decided on a career as a reporter. In his short thirty-four years he had covered almost every major war on the planet. He was a war correspondent and considered himself the greatest correspondent that ever lived. He had written one book and with the royalties he bought out every drug and liquor store south of Market—cases of Rainier Ale (or Green Death as he liked to call it) and boxes of amyl nitrite which he used to get his heart started every morning because coffee didn't work any more. He was a wild man and a crazy man and he had taken every drug in the book, smoked it and ate it and snorted it. He had tripped hundreds of times on acid, and where many others of a lesser constitution and strength would have succumbed and surely by now fried their brains completely out, Daniels miraculously maintained his health. Though he looked like hell and death warmed over when you saw him close up, and all the people who knew him wondered in amazement that he could keep going and bingeing and ingesting, chasing wildly and frantically for wars and more wars with his dirty books stuffed in his back pocket and his baseball cards and bounced checks and rumpled shirts and Salvation Army

49

jackets, fiercely he moved through life, nothing stopping him nothing holding him back, challenging anything and anybody that got in his way. He had no rules, no boundaries, no laws, no church, no God, no country—just himself bold and brave and free, pouring and blasting, roaring at a thousand million miles an hour through life, gas pedal to the floor no brakes no restraints getting all he could as fast as he could, drinking drugging getting laid getting fucked getting screwed getting humped getting pumped. He was phenomenal.

He was amazing. He kept going burning roaring like an enormous rocket always threatening to explode, always just about to blow, blinding you with his light his energy his tolerance for anything and everything. He was unstoppable. He could not be contained. He charmed women with fabulous stories of his revolutions and wars and dangerous trips with the border guards and the IRA and in Lebanon and El Salvador and everywhere. Everywhere. He wanted life, he wanted all of it, everything he could get his hands on, and now now now and not a minute later. Life was this moment for Daniels screaming and yelling and pulsating driving and driving with everything he had in him with all he possessed or would ever possess. He wanted wanted wanted and he got got got almost everything. Yes, he burned burned burned like a raging comet out of control, spinning wildly and recklessly, a mad roller coaster ride through the twentieth century, defying all logic, abiding by no rules but his own and even pulling his own teeth down in Mexico once with his shoe lace and a door knob. He was his own doctor, his own lawyer and shrink and "better to have a bottle in front of you than a frontal lobotomy," he'd always say with a wild and manic laugh.

I had first met him years before when he was on the run from a bad-check-writing spree. He had lived in nineteen houses in two months, had eleven cars and eight different girlfriends in three states. Yes, he was really crazy back then. And after years of traveling nonstop and furious abuse of his body and mind, Daniels, with a loan of $58 from his father who had just had a stroke and didn't know what to do with his money any more, caught a bus back to his beloved San Francisco just in time for the Super Bowl which he really loved. He'd even interrupt his coverage of a war to return home to watch. The Super Bowl was history as far as Daniels was concerned. It was as important as any war he ever covered or any woman he ever slept with. He had great reverence for the Super Bowl. It was American and red white and blue and he loved it loved it loved it and danced and sang and got drunk and stoned out of his mind popping valiums, or vals as he liked to call them, like they were candy. He'd jump into his broken-down V8 Charger right after the game was over. The Last Great American Car on the Planet he called it, revving up the engine until it sounded like it was going to burst, then racing it squealing rubber a long wild incredible patch, roaring out across the Golden Gate Bridge at a hundred miles an hour with his broken speedometer reading zero, his famous white-knuckles-ride all the way to the tunnel where the rainbow is over in Marin then back again pushing the V8 for everything it was worth, swigging down large quantities of Green Death and popping and snorting amyl nitrites just as the sunset exploded like a flaming orange yellow curtain shimmering along the Pacific horizon like a great showcase. His eyes burned fiercely. He coughed, he hacked his emphysema-wracked lungs, and pulled his little black phone book out of his pocket desperate for a woman. He hated sleeping alone. He had fathered children all over the planet and had wives and lovers left scattered everywhere, but still he wanted more more more, there was never enough time never enough people air space pussy dope more more more war death violence, excitement torture glory life life incessant unrelenting mad and crazy wild and nonstop adventure after adventure. He beamed with excitment, he lit up with excitement.

Oh wonderful life! Beautiful life! All the possibilities all the people the things to do the places to go and now and not a moment later, for Daniels loved the crazy ones, the wild ones not afraid to live, the ones that kept moving and going and doing and being, the ones that sizzled and simmered and rapped until dawn, flirting and kissing and hugging and loving knowing that this was it and all there would ever be and you had to make the most of it and every second counted and there wasn't anything more important in the world than being alive and knowing it.

"The Great American Hero."

I could see Richie was inspired by the challenge. He stood there as if he were about to give a great speech.

"I'll build a rocket and go out into space," he proclaimed. "Because I'm the King! The world is my palace. I own everything I own nothing. I'm Jesus in a stinking robe. I'm Jesus with alcoholic breath. I'm weaving, marching down Polk Street in my dirty underwear."

"In his Salvation Army jacket," I added. "In his garbage can shoes with his Green Death and his scratching and his pills and his cortisone and his rashes and his snoring."

"With his football," shouted Richie, jumping up on the coffee table, "and his Super Bowl and his mercenaries," he shouted again, his voice at a feverish pitch.

"His love affairs and his baseball cards and Nazi war songs choking on LSD," murmured the Chief in his sleep.

"Swimming the San Francisco Bay," shouted Richie, diving off the coffee table and back onto the couch.

"Richie, Richie, my friend Richie," I said as if I was introducing an act in a show. "My friend Richie, off to another war, off to another conquest, a woman, some foreign land, some comic book in Africa deep below the jungle in filthy glasses in loaded rifles in dives in suicide notes in the gutters dirty filthy friends rundown houses beat-up cars rumpled clothing bloodshot eyes. Richie, Richie in Kansas in Chicago in Beirut in San Salvador in the Amazon with my dog in Berlin and Belfast in Cambodia and Chattanooga yes Chattanooga with a sleigh and bells and bobtails and glimmers of expectancy on the San Francisco Bay..."

"Three days?" Richie paused with a serious look on his face. "No problem, man." He cleared his throat. "I know just the man for the job."

"I knew you'd know who could help me get the rest of the way around the world."

"Sure, sure," said Richie. "Don't worry." He took another healthy swig from his beer bottle. "I know a million people in this town. It's a holy city. It's got magic, but you just have to know how to find it." He suddenly frowned and bounced his beer bottle off the wall.

"Good shot, Richie!" I said.

"Yeah, I never miss," said Rich.

"Never?" said the Chief starting to wake up on the floor.

"Well, almost never," said Richie, looking down at the Chief.

We raced out into the San Francisco morning. It was bright and beautiful, and the wind which swept up from the hills was cool and it made all of us feel so wonderful and alive and like there was still hope. We jumped into Richie's broken down V8 Charger and raced down Sutter Street making a quick right on Polk.

"Where we going?" I asked.

"Doc's place," said Richie. "He's the only person on the planet right now who can help you."

The V8 engine strained for everything it was worth as we drove to the very top of Pacific Heights where all the rich and famous people of San Francisco live. You could see the whole city from up there and even the Chief said it took his breath away.

"Wow," said the Chief, who stared at the fog and great expanse of orange metal and steel that was the great Golden Gate Bridge and Marin all green and lush and smelling of eucalyptus trees, even at seven thousand yards. There were islands and Alcatraz and sea gulls and prison breaks and helicopters and the soft soothing fog that swept up haphazardly perpendicular to right angles and old photographs of Market Street and Montgomery and Polk and Hyde and Sutter. We were in the Heights in the clouds above the Bay the great water the lake the beautiful bay leading to the great and awesome Pacific, in our sandals and our beads and our peace pipes reminiscing with our smiles and smell of exhaust fumes and tobacco smoke and dope and peyote and mushrooms. Our heads were spinning and we saw God and we danced and jitterbugged on Richie's car and took turns being the hood ornament. The wind flew and we fastened ourselves to the air, we joyrided in space for a while. I looked. I circled with my head alive so incredibly alive like spring and daffodils.

"And exploding turkeys," insisted the Chief bowing now in some strange ritual on the roof of Richie's car in a way neither Rich nor myself could understand.

"Does that have something to do with God?" I asked the Chief.

"Flypaper," said the Chief softly. "Flypaper and onions."

We were home, even the Chief; yet, even so, I thought we had arrived. I must have been only joking because we were leaving, departing in the twinkle of an eye—on a journey that had no beginning nor end.

Three men, a mistress and a rummage sale a machine of time we sat atop the world that morning atop San Francisco looking out on a trip that sat timeless in space balanced on a very sharp razor.

Richie started up the car again and a few minutes later after a wild ride across the Oakland Bay Bridge, the Charger and all the Chief's false front teeth vibrating madly. We arrived at Doc's place. Doctor Twist, the famous Professor of Rock and Roll and one of the most interesting and informed men on the face of the planet. Everyone had heard of Doctor Twist.

Doc was one of the most respected musicologists in the city. For years he had been the famous Doctor Twist and it had been only recently that he'd decided to leave his profession for something different. For some reason yet to be understood or explained, he had left his job at radio station KYC where he did the Golden Oldies Doctor Twist show for years, telling everybody he was getting married, buying a dog, and moving to Russia—none of which he did.

For a long time the good doctor had told his friends that he wanted to go to Europe where he didn't have to live in crazy America any more.

"They'll like me in Europe," Doc told his friends. "I'll be a big star in Amsterdam. I'll get laid every night and twice on Tuesday." And so when he quit his job at the radio station, everybody believed he was going to Russia. But the word had quickly filtered back to town that Doc hadn't left for Europe at all, and after throwing a wild and lavish party where two teenage girls lost their virginity and hundreds of old Beatle records and stereo cassettes got smashed, Doc fooled people into thinking he was going to the airport the next morning while actually he headed for a secret bungalow in Berkeley where he began work on his Fantastic Time Machine.

"His fantastic what?" I asked Richie as we walked up the steps to Doc's place.

"A Time Machine," said Richie with a serious look on his face. "He's invented a machine that splices time, and makes mincemeat out of hours and seconds. It slashes the tick, and dissects the tock of a clock."

"Amazing!" I shouted.

"Not so loud," said Richie. "Doc's probably still sleeping. He stays up every night." Richie knocked on Doc's door which was old and made of oak and covered with ivy.

"What a beautiful door," I said to Richie, pulling the Chief along behind me by his hand. "Come on, Chief."

"It'll take me weeks to recover from this," said the Chief.

"Months," said Richie with a little laugh. "Don't worry, you'll be all right, just hang in there."

The door finally opened and there was Doctor Twist pretty much the same as I always remembered him to be in his Doctor Twist outfit with his twisted tie hanging from his neck. He seemed a bit older than the last time I'd seen him down in Santa Cruz when he was going with a beautiful black woman named Carol and still talking about being the most famous DJ in America. His hair had grayed a bit, and where once before there had been a bright happy sparkle in his eyes, there now was just a serious look that made me realize almost immediately how much Doctor Twist had changed.

57

"Doc, how ya doin'," I said, happy to see my old friend again. "Hey, Doc, this is my friend the Chief. Chief, this is my friend Doctor Twist. The Chief drove me all the way from Tucson on his motorcycle after he and his friends attacked our broken-down car. The Chief's really a great guy. He's been through a lot, just like all the rest of us in America."

"A real road warrior," said Richie with a jealous snarl and for a second it looked like Richie and the Chief were going to fight, but at the last second the Chief backed down when Richie challenged him to a game of Knucks where each guy punches the other guy as hard as he can, trying to break his knuckles.

"I'd rather play him at chess," said the Chief. "I'm quite good at chess."

I continued asking Doc questions about his new Time Machine and begged him to show me where it was. I told him I had less than three days to get around the world, and all about Bobby Thompson and the bet I had made and how five days had already elapsed and I still had to cover well over 22,000 miles in less than seventy-two hours.

"Impossible!" said the Chief.

"I don't think you can do it, not without an airplane or a rocket or something," said Richie.

"No way," I told him. "I can't use a plane or a rocket or a jet or any of those things. I've got to make it around the world some other way."

"There's got to be a force field involved," said Doctor Twist. "A musical force field with Skitch Henderson and Beethoven and Bach. There's got to be rhythm, harmony and a few broken chords melded together with a little soul music. Yes, there's got to be piccolos playing and two guys named Pete, Russian symphonies and Norwegian wood."

"Loud pianos, too," suggested Richard.

"And drums, forty sets of drums—Gene Krupa!" insisted the Chief.

"Yeah. And Ella Fitzgerald and Morey Amsterdam," I added.

"Drums!" shouted the Chief again, angrily, "there's got to be more drums."

"OK, OK," said Doctor Twist, stepping toward the Chief. "We'll have a three-piece band, mind-bending music played with a tomahawk, two Indianhead nickels and a wounded buffalo."

"That's crazy," I said.

"You're damn right," said Doctor Twist. It's wild it's nuts it's rock it's blues mixed with a little glee."

"Oh, yeah, Oh, yeah," said the Chief getting into the beat, pounding his enormous hands on Doc's collar. "TV. Boom Boom Boom Boom Bow," he began to chant.

"It's gonna take a lot to get there," said Doctor Twist more serious than before. "It's gonna take . . . "

There was a long pause and at that moment a beautiful woman in a long and flowing white dress with a spectacular red rose pinned right above her heart appeared in front of us. "Carmen," I said in amazement. It was Carmen, the woman I had met at the bus station, the beautiful exchange student from Brazil. "Carmen, what are you doing here?" I asked. "What happened to you? You got off the bus at that stop. I thought you were getting back on and I just

59

closed my eyes for a minute and then you were gone. What happened to you?"

I still found it hard to believe that the same woman who had been riding with me on the bus to Kansas City was now standing before me as beautiful and stunning as she had been a few days before at the Miranda Greyhound bus depot.

"How is your lip, señor?" she asked. She walked toward me and touched my mouth gently with her finger.

"Oh, it's OK, it's all healed up," I said, touching it myself to see how it was doing. For a moment we stood there staring into each other's eyes. She was beautiful. God, she was beautiful.

"How did you ever get here to Doctor Twist's place?" I asked her. But she said nothing and winked her eye as a grin just for a moment appeared on her face.

"Well, who cares. What does it matter, we're all here together, Carmen," I said grabbing her wrist gently. "This is my friend Richard Daniels. He's from San Francisco, and this is my friend the Chief," I said pointing towards the Chief who was sitting in the corner. "He's one of the most amazing men I've ever met." Richie made a funny sound with his mouth just as I said that, but the Chief remained still, his legs crossed and his back now straight as a board. "Besides killing and scalping this crazy cowboy who picked me up," I continued, "outside of Tucson he was kind enough to give me a ride on his motorcycle all the way into town. The bike's at the bottom of a swimming pool right now, but me and the Chief are OK and that's all that matters. Isn't that right?" I said, looking over at the Chief.

"Sure," said the Chief, a bit depressed and a little out of it.

"He's OK," I said to Carmen, apologizing for his behavior. "He's tired from the trip. He'll be all right in a while."

And then, just as I went to introduce Carmen to Doctor Twist, the Doctor stepped forward and put his arm around Carmen. He pulled her closely to his side.

"What's up, man," I shouted. "What's going on here?" I was feeling a little bit jealous and angry at Doc for moving in and getting so close the woman I'd fallen completely in love with only days before.

"Hey, cool it, man," said Doctor Twist. "Just keep your cool and everything's gonna be OK." The Doctor then leaned over toward beautiful Carmen, kissing her passionately and crazily on the lips which he tried to open repeatedly with the Doctor Twist lollypops he always carried in his pocket. "Come on, open wide," shouted the Doctor as he tried to get the lollypop down sweet little Carmen's throat. "Come on, come on you sweet little Mexican thing." But no matter how hard Doctor Twist tried to get Carmen to make out with him, she refused. She was still faithful to me. My girl.

"Oh, I've got sunshine on a cloudy day, I've even got the month of May," I sang. "Talkin bout talkin bout my girl," I sang. I breathed a sigh of relief, looking at Richie and the Chief for support.

"I'd punch him in the nose if I were you," said the Chief. "I saw a man do that to my woman once," said the Chief standing up, "and I kicked him in the balls."

"Yeah, why don't you do something," shouted Richie, making a fist. "I'd knock any guy's block off who would mess with my lady. I'd say the Doctor was trespassing on your property," said Richie, slapping his fist again and again against his open hand.

"Well, I just met her for the first time the other day. She's not really my girl," I said sort of backing down from a fight. "I really didn't want to get involved in the first place. Hey," I said looking over at Carmen and Doctor Twist, "do whatever you want."

"It's your movie, man," shouted Richie.

"Yeah, I guess so," I said still looking at Carmen and the Doctor. "Do your thing, man. It's your fucking movie . . . I just want to get around the world and back to Massapequa to collect Bobby Thompson and his father's life savings and I've got less than three days left."

"OK," said Doctor Twist. "That's what I was waiting for."

"What do you mean, that's what you were waiting for," I said wondering what Doctor Twist was talking about.

"He was testing you," shouted the Chief.

"Testing the living shit out of you," shouted Richie.

"He was trying to see if you would crack," said Carmen now, walking toward me with a big smile and gently kissing me on the cheek. "He wanted to know."

"He wanted to know what?" I asked.

"Know if you really wanted it," said the Chief.

"Wanted what," I said.

"Wanted the trip," said the Chief.

"The trip?" I said.

"Yes, the trip," said Doctor Twist, "the trip through

time and space into a musical note on a wall of colorful spinning dials and dots."

"And a farewell to all that," shouted the Chief.

"A dance of dunces a dangerous domino a whole slew of kisses and stanzas," shouted Carmen.

"A trip to the stars and the moon, but not too soon," said Doctor Twist.

"A roar of a tiger at a gate and a lake kept half awake," said the Chief softly pulling out his peace pipe.

"Yes, a trip," said Richie, "a trip to Dixieland to the sun sand and trees and five bees on their knees slurping gravy and wiping their sleeves."

"Yes," said Doctor Twist,"white bobby socks and Dick Clark brass rings and robin sings."

"Trench coats, and dark grey tunnels too," crooned Richie.

"Every road, and all roads," said Carmen.

"The Yellow Brick Road?" I shouted.

"Yes," said Doctor Twist with a big smile. "The Yellow Brick Road."

"And Toto too!" howled the Chief.

"And Toto too,"said Doctor Twist matter-of-factly.

"Get your baggage," said Richie.

"All you need is yourself to come on board," said Carmen pressing close to me.

"When do we leave?" I asked, looking at Doctor Twist.

"We've already left," whispered the Doctor putting his index finger to his lips as if to say for all of us to be quiet.

"OK, OK, we're gone," I said, "we're gone somewhere."

"Everywhere and anywhere," said Carmen squeezing my arm tightly.

"Are we going to Kansas?" I said.

"No, you've already been to Kansas," said the Chief.

"You're going much deeper, much further," said Doctor Twist. "You're going under, deeply under and far removed from all and every."

"Sort of a local anesthesia," said Richie.

"Up and over and under and sideways," said the Doctor. "Deep deep deep and beyond and before . . . before anything, beyond anything."

"Better than best but bitter and butter," I said.

"Sort of," said the Chief, "but more mostly than mainly than mustard and jam."

"Oh, I see," I said not yet really understanding but wanting to try hard to travel with them.

"You must be, but not be, but better you begin by being better," said the Doctor bending over and picking up a speck of dust off the very tips of his shoes.

"You cause your own alarms on this trip," said the Chief.

"You signal when you're hurt," said Carmen who was trying to help me understand what the Chief had just said.

"You rotate to and fro like this," said Doctor Twist

sort of twisting in front of me. "See, you move and when you move the alarm is set off."

"Seven alarms are set off," said Richie.

"Everyone will hear them," said Carmen, "and we will know it's time to help you. The Indians in the Amazon say there is no time in truth, the truth is in dreaming. They travel far and deep."

The night became dark and it split in fours, somersaulting through a glass window that shattered in an angry spiral of hail turned to dust and wind and everything to think again so close and lost like drifting snow of December heat wave sprinkles I say flutters of spiral birthday cakes entwined in seeds and mumbletypegs shale and sheet rock too.

"Enormous breaths! You must take enormous breaths," shouted the Doctor. "You must breathe as if you could see. You must take most if not every all and other nots of what and when. Force it," said the Doctor.

"Force it!" screamed the Chief.

"And lightning will strike Madrid," said Carmen softly.

"Make it a happy thought a long and lasting see-through thought a counterpunch to a long trial against the wind a soft soothing thing, a lightning bolt made of rubber," said Richie.

"Rubber?" I asked.

"Yes, a torch, a light, anything that awakes the heart," Doctor Twist whispered.

"Anything that can be sold for rubies," said Carmen, now raising her voice.

"Portugal!" I cried.

"No, not yet," said Doctor Twist. "Portugal is later and definitely much too soon."

"It is December," said the Chief. "December in the wigwams and there are fires."

"We're in Denver," I said.

"No, Denver, is gone," said Doctor Twist.

"We are in December," said Carmen.

"And there are palm trees and wigwams," said the Chief sounding sad.

"There are valleys and sunsets, beautiful sunsets," said Richie.

"There are umbrellas," said Carmen softly, "umbrellas and people in love."

"That sounds beautiful," I said.

"It sounds American," said Doctor Twist.

"American and December with snow and fires," said the Chief. Cardboard ... miracles stretched out for miles, members of religious sects crossing over to the other side." He lit his peace pipe.

"Religious factions," said the Doctor.

"Sects," said the Chief, taking a puff on his pipe.

"Factions, friction and fraternity brothers, fat ones," said Richie.

"Yes, fat ones with brothers, oh yes sisters too, on sleds on the tops of the palm trees," I shouted.

"Yes," said Doctor Twist, "many men thinking differently."

"And women too," said Carmen.

"Women with crosses," said the Chief.

"And thorns," said Richie. "Mile-long thorns made in Ann Arbor, Michigan.

"Packed in Poughkeepsie,"said Carmen.

66

"Shipped from Susquehanna," sang the Chief.

"Overland to Oswego," said Doctor Twist.

"Catapulted to California," said Richie.

"Yes," said Doctor Twist, "twist on the floor in front of me, just move like this ... "

"And we will know," whispered Carmen in my ear.

"Hawaii," I shouted, "it's Hawaii, isn't it?"

"No," said Doctor Twist with a little giggle. "It just *was* Hawaii."

"Oh," I said, reaching in the darkness for Carmen's hand. "Carmen! Carmen! Where are you Carmen?"

"She's over there," said the Chief. "Over where?" I said, looking into the darkness.

"At right angles too," said Doctor Twist firmly.

"Under," said Richie. "She had virgin eyes. Her father was brave."

"He was a soldier," I shouted. "A sailor?"

"He was a farmer," said Carmen in a soft voice.

"A poor farmer," said the Chief.

"Kansas City," I shouted.

"We passed it," said the Chief.

"He was a brave man," said Carmen's voice.

"Carmen, Carmen—where are you, Carmen?"

"He stood up to the big landowners and the big bosses," said Doctor Twist.

"He would not give in," said Carmen.

"He saw an opportunity for a better world," said Doctor Twist.

"For a community where they cared about one another," said the Chief with a touch of sorrow in his voice.

"He saw the future on a Tuesday," said Carmen.

"He saw it in a vacuum," said Richie.

"In a thimble," said the Chief, puffing his pipe.

"In a puff," said Doctor Twist, "in a puff of time."

"He resisted!" I cried out.

"They chained him, ankles and wrist, neck and thick suntanned shoulders. They crucified him," said Carmen.

"Under the earth," said Doctor Twist, "with the maggots and the flies."

"With the Indians," said Carmen.

"In Brazil," said the Chief.

"By the stovepipes and filthy huts by the river by the river where the blood still flows and their graves are still fresh," said Carmen.

"Warm," said Doctor Twist, "warm with resistance and love for humankind."

"Humility," I said.

"No," said Doctor Twist, "warm, just warm with love."

It grew dark and it wished and it wished some more. It was tranquil.

"Turkey," I cried.

"No, not yet," said the Doctor. "I feel the heat," said the Chief. "Heat and stench and buzzing flies. It's colorful," said Richie.

"Like a rainbow," said Carmen, a little uneasy.

"Hammers," I said.

"Yes, hammers," said Doctor Twist, "two hammers."

"And a flash and a kick like a mule," said the Chief.

"Yes, and murderous screams," said Richie.

"And children crying," cried Carmen.

"Twine times of most many burnt better butter and toast," cried the Doctor.

"Burnt tongues," I shouted.

"Yes," said the Chief. "Like the wigwams."

"On a Tuesday," said Carmen.

"Yes, on a Tuesday ankle deep in soot and fire," said the Doctor.

"I feel uncomfortable. There's got to be a lot of easier ways to get around the world than this. I don't like this at all," I said. Maybe we could just stop this for a while. It was fun, but I don't like it any more. We could go around the world a lot of other ways. We could go down to LA in Richie's cousin's car, all of us, and in LA we can all grab the tails of a school of dolphins that would suddenly appear to us while we were walking on the beach. The dolphins would go over two-hundred miles an hour and they'd be real friendly and intelligent and they'd know all about Bobby Thompson and his father and the bet and they'd take us to Hawaii and in Hawaii we'd get attacked by the Japanese and the Chief would save us all," I said, crying now.

"The Chief would be a big hero with Richie. They'd find us a submarine and we'd go really fast, ten-thousand miles an hour in that submarine," I pleaded. "There'd be nobody stopping us all the way to Japan and then there'd be some kind of huge catapult on the top of Fujiyama and everybody would be waiting for us and we'd all get in this little cup and whammo they'd shoot the thing and we'd wake up in Paris with bruises all over us but we'd just be hours away from Massapequa. And some rich entrepreneur would hire us aboard his speedboat that did eight-hundred miles an hour before it even warmed up and we'd split the ocean in two and have time for a picnic lunch half way across the Atlantic, then we'd make it back to my home town and that's all there'd be to it. Don't you think, Chief? Doctor? Don't you think that would be a lot better idea than this? It's just too confusing. So why don't we just switch stations on this Time Machine? We're probably still in Berkeley anyway, aren't we? I love Berkeley. It's a beautiful place, especially in the spring. Everything smells so beautiful in Berkeley and the girls down on Sproul Plaza are so pretty. Can't we just do it a different way, Doctor? A way that's easier, a way that's not so hard? You know what I mean. I feel I might have made a mistake, you know, like somebody who gets on a plane that's gonna crash and he doesn't know it's gonna crash. Is anyone listening? Is anyone listening to me?"

The song "Watusi" started playing. "Come on and take a chance and get a with it stance. Watusi makes you feel so good, Oh baby it's a dance made for Romance ... Baby baby that's the way it goes, nothing happens when you mash potato." Everybody started singing and dancing. I reached for Carmen's hand. I thought of high school for a moment and the day everybody was signing each other's year books. Boy, that was a neat day, I thought, everybody wrote such nice things in my book. We kept dancing for a while, doing the Watusi as best we could until we got pretty tired, and then all of a sudden Doctor Twist put his hand up in the air and the song "Wake Up Little Susie" started playing full blast. "What're you gonna tell you ma, what're gonna tell your pa. Wake up Little Susie, Wake up ... " The song went on and on. It began to fade more and more.

"With wristbands?" asked the Chief.

"No with ballbearings and live wires," said the Doctor.

"With cap pistols and molten steel with flash burns and eyes frozen shut," said the Chief.

"Melted shut," shouted the Doctor.

"Japan," I said, reaching for Carmen. "Carmen? Where are you Carmen?"

"With hair falling out," said Carmen softly.

"On a Tuesday?" I asked.

"Yes," said Carmen, "a Tuesday."

"With bad well water," said the Chief.

"And blankets with diseases in them," said the Doctor.

"Bubonic plague?" I said.

"Much worse," said the Chief.

"Hair falling out," said Carmen. The song "Soldier Boy" started playing all of a sudden. "Soldier boy, you were my first love and you'll be my last love. I'll be true to you cause I love you so ... I'll be true to you, take my love with you to any foreign shore ... soldier boy, oh my little soldier boy, I'll be true to you."

"In El Salvador," said the Doctor.

"In Brazil," said the Chief. "Forests falling, tribes vanishing."

"Japan!" I screamed. The time passed but it didn't pass like an eagle's wing. It fluttered succinctly scattering its afterthoughts in deep and ever-present terrors death and time passing, moments fading to dust in darkness and nothing in never in not in never not yes tips and colors of a rainbow present on a colorful wheel. Deeper and deeper we went into time then and lost things shaking and shimmering into families that once were then never again then gone, then facing east, then west, on fire and screaming ...

"Japan," I said softly. "Japan and balsawood airplanes in my grandmother Mary's backyard."

"No, airplanes," said the Chief.

"They're not allowed," said the Doctor.

"Only moving and music," said Richie.

"Faster and harder," said Carmen.

"Oh, Carmen," I said, almost crying.

"There Ain't No Cure for the Summertime Blues" started playing, an angry hard rock song. "Sometimes I wonder what I'm goin' to do, oh, there ain't no cure for the summertime blues." The music grew louder and louder, more and more intense, the guitars sounded like they were going to explode, everything was roaring. "I've got to take my problems to the United Nations ... sometimes I wonder what I'm gonna do, Lord, there ain't no cure for the summertime blues ... "

Carmen and I swayed to the song. "That was The Who," I said to Carmen. Carmen looked over at Doctor Twist. "The river," I said.

"In Brazil," said the Chief, who told me he liked The Who too.

"In El Salvador," said the Doctor.

I continued swaying back and forth, Carmen at my side. It felt so wonderful to be close to someone again. She smelled so good and I felt myself relax and breathe and sigh deeply. I wondered why I never had the nerve to go out with girls when I was in high school. It always happens this way, I thought to myself, feeling sad. Nothing happens for months and years, and then all of a sudden you decide to go on the road and you meet somebody just like that. It's so crazy sometimes, I thought.

The music stopped, and I couldn't feel Carmen any more.

"Carmen?" I said.

"She went fishing," said the Chief. "Down to the river." I was beginning to feel dark again but just as he said that, the great old song, "Johnny Be Good" started blasting. "He used to carry his guitar in a gunny sack. Oh, go go go Johnny go ... oh go go Johnny be good ... " The guitar in the song wailed and then, "Maybe some day your name will be in lights, saying Johnny be good tonight." It was a wild and crazy song that drove through the night madly and chopped kicking notes and crazily screamed again and again.

"Carmen? Carmen?"

"That was the great Chuck Berry in Johnny Be Good!" There was Doctor Twist's voice again.

"Oh, yeah," said the Chief, "I danced my first dance in high school to that song."

"Really," said Richie, almost sarcastically. "I got laid for the first time to the last stanza of that song."

"The whole country got laid to that song," said the Doctor, "but I want you to listen to this one." The Doctor turned the music up full blast. It was Bob Dylan's "Like a Rolling Stone." "Now you don't talk

73

so loud, now you don't seem so proud about having to be scrounging your next meal . . . how does it feel, how does it feel to be without a home like a complete unknown, like a rolling stone . . ." The harmonica was wonderful and we all swayed . . . racing through space and time. "You're invisible now, you ain't got no secrets to conceal, how does it feel, how does it feel . . ." We all sang together louder and louder, Dylan's harmonica blasting in our ears. "Oh, Dylan," I cried. "He's so beautiful."

"China," I shouted.

"Peking," said the Doctor.

"No way," said Richie.

"I want to hear more music," demanded the Chief. "I love the music," he said banging on Doctor Rock's color TV. "Alabama," he laughed.

"Doctor Twist turned the little dial and the wonderful song "I'm Walking" started playing. We all started dancing crazily again, beating and bouncing to the great beat. "I'm walkin' . . . I'm hopin' that you'll come back to me." It was a wild party and soon I lost my breath and felt exhausted.

"Carmen, Carmen, you're my high school date. You're the girl I never took to the senior prom." I reached out to touch her beautiful soft skin. "Oh, Carmen, Christ Jesus, please Carmen touch me again, touch me, hold me and dance with me the way we were dancing before." I felt dizzy and thought I was going to faint. The music kept getting louder and louder and it was dark and I felt lost and lonely and afraid.

"Keep the music playing." I said, remembering all

the times when I was a boy and frightened in my room in the middle of the dark dark night and mom and dad would be sleeping in their beds and I'd turn on my little transistor radio I always kept under my pillow so I wouldn't be so lonely. And I'd listen to the news to see what was happening in the world and then I'd turn the little plastic dial to the songs that I listened to all night.

"Like this?!" asked Doctor Twist, twisting the dial again to another station. "I Love a Place Where We Can Go" was playing ... " It was a beautiful old song and reminded me of so many wonderful times when I was young.

"All around there are girls and boys, a swinging place with a cellar full of noise. I know a place where we can go." The beat was beautiful and I hadn't felt happier on the whole trip. "I know a place where the music is fine and the lights are always low. I know a place where we can go ... I know a place where we can go ... "

Then came the song "Ferry 'Cross the Mersey" and we all sat back and relaxed for a while. Richie lit up a joint, and the Chief kept puffing on his peace pipe. It was a mellow moment, and Carmen was back in my arms snuggled up close to me.

"I love this," I said to Carmen. "What a wonderful way to go around the world."

"Yeah," said Carmen, almost purring now like a pussy cat.

"Alabama," laughed the Chief, laying his peace pipe down.

"The Crimson Tide. The heart of the Confederacy," whispered the Doctor.

"The turning point in the war," I said.

"Exactly," said the Doctor. He turned up the dial.

"Here we go again," I screamed with glee, absolute glee. "I've got my girl, who could ask for anything more, trouble I don't mind it ... I got sweet dreams, I got my girl, who could ask for more." The trumpets blasted dip dip dip dip ... "old man trouble I don't mind him ... I've got rhythm, I've got music, I've got my girl ... "

"This is the dawning of the age of Aquarius ..." the next song came on. "Harmony and understanding, trust abounding, mystic crystal revelations Aquarius Aquarius ... when the moon is in the seventh house and Jupiter aligns with Mars ... Let the sun shine, let the sun shine in, let the sun shine, oh, let it shine, the sun shine in, open up your heart, you've got to feel it ohhhh, the sun shine in let the sun shine in, I want you to sing along, open up your heart." All of us joined in.

"The turning point of the war," I said.

"Ulysses S. Grant," said Carmen.

"She's gone fishing," said the Doctor.

"Fishing," said the Chief.

"Not China, then?" I said.

"Maybe," said the Doctor.

"Maybe what?" I asked.

"Maybe not China," said the Doctor. "Maybe difficulties. Maybe not China at all," said the Doctor firmly.

"I remember a fountain pen in high school that talked back to me once," I shouted. "The wind then blew and raindrops as big as hail and stones flying from angry mobs in the streets of Madrid!" I shouted.

"Too soon," said the Doctor patiently.

"Japan!" I cried, exhausted.

"We've passed it," said the Doctor. "Didn't you see the smoke?"

"You pushed the button," said the Chief.

"You saw Jersey in the bombsights," said Carmen.

"Carmen," I cried.

"You saw women and children on the trolleys," said the Doctor.

"Play the music. Play the music!" I demanded.

"You took advantage of their innocence," shouted Richie.

"What are you talking about, Richie? Why don't you just pop a couple of amyl nitrites and smoke a joint. Take a ride over the Golden Gate Bridge. Why don't you go up to Coit Tower and get it on with some poor girl you were in love with in high school and who was really brilliant and went crazy, and she's been in and out of the nut house and living on the streets and sleeping in the gutters and she smells of piss and you know she's gonna die. Why don't you call her up, if she has a phone, and drag her down from her crummy flop house ... "

"It was on a Tuesday," said Carmen.

"I did nothing!" I insisted.

"You took advantage," shouted the Chief.

"What is this, some kind of fucking trial?" I shouted angrily.

"You rearranged their molecules," said Richie angrily.

"I'm getting hurt," I cried.

"You're getting closer," said the Doctor.

"I'm getting angry," I said. "I'm getting very angry. I remember when you slept on a chaise lounge, Doctor Twist, out on some guy's porch in Berkeley because you were so broke. You were popping ludes all the time and you were sick and pathetic and your dog had just died down in L.A. Chubby, your dog who you loved and everybody loved," I screamed, lashing out at the Doctor any way I could. "You got that dog killed. You let him run free, you got him sent to the gas chamber. You kept talking about suicide, Doctor Twist. You wanted to die and leave this miserable rotten stinking world.

"Yeah, I'm getting angry, at all of you. Who do you think you are? What do you think you're doing to me?"

"Inhale," said the Chief. "The smoke is thick."

"It's acrid," said the Doctor.

"It's hot, very hot," said Carmen.

"Japan! Japan! Japan!" I cried again and again.

"It's too late," said the Doctor.

"It's December," said the Chief.

"No, Tuesday," said Carmen.

"In the wigwams," cried the Chief. "In the wigwams."

"We move now," said the Doctor. "Definitely. We move through high above where deafening mushroom clouds of sick and shrapnel still descend on Denver."

"In December," said the Chief.

"In Detroit," said Richie.

"And Duluth," said Carmen wiping tears from her eyes.

"Carmen," I said softly.

"In Delaware," said Carmen.

"In December," I said.

"In the dark," said the Doctor.

The room began to rumble and there was a great flash of light that blinded me and threw me to the floor with tremendous force. The room swirled and tore violently apart sideways. The Chief disintegrated before my eyes, and Carmen became a skeleton, her long hair afire and roaring like an inferno. I smelled her burning skin, melting wax down her face that held one single agonizing second of a scream.

"Doctor Twist stood there, then suddenly evaporated into yellowish dust. Richie was a flaming puddle of molten skin and bones, black and charred like the walls of the room that were no more. I saw a great screen descend before what I could still watch with my eyes I had in my body and mind still somehow there to see all these things. The great screen of death and darkness so bleak and cold I at first could not watch, but upward my chin and face were thrust by forces and powers as demonic as frightening. I had to look. Someone or something was making me see.

The lights shone and exactly at that moment the cries and screams of a million headless children wandering the world naked, in tattered clothing burnt flesh, screaming like frightened animals in the darkness of this doom and time. The great screen flickered and passed in review, my mother whom I loved screaming hysterical naked raped by war, a mad woman in chains that burned and seared her flesh that had given birth in years long since past. She jumped off the screen, her hair singed to the roots, unrecognizable, my mother in hell, in flaming apron dress scarred and charred human mother asking why with her eyes melted tightly together like her lips dead. My mother, my mother, I cried as she disappeared off the screen howling like a banshee, lost lonely and afraid. Everything gone, everything lost, suddenly without warning, shockingly. My father then appeared, frozen like a statue. Stiffly he walked, like a dead man, his eyes fixed vacantly in the distance staggering, still shielding his eyes from the blast, naked like my mother, shot back into time back to the caves and the beginning. My father's face about to scream frozen forever like this. Forever in hell and agony, his fingers singed off, his ears clipped off and disfigured and the sound of the children still screaming and wailing as if all being murdered at once with one angry terrible blast of a gun. My father staggers into the distance, into nowhere. My brothers, my sisters. I recognize all of their faces. They follow each other like blind mice, their eyes all of them shut and burned and melted shut. Their hands frozen together in shock of the trauma of that moment. I remember all the times we spent growing up together. I hear the screams. My brothers and sisters cannot scream any longer. Their faces all melted like my father's in one hellish twist of anger frightened and frozen like a particle of still nothing. They walk around in a circle as if trying to find a place to kneel down and pray with their fingertips all white and their eye sockets as deep and dark as the night around me. They walk into the distance, my brothers and my sisters. I am crying now. I miss them and want to be with them but the flash and the night have taken them away to die in some ditch stinking from decay, the blast that hit them in their sleep when they were peaceful.

And the town is on the screen now, Massapequa. I know it so well, but all is gone now, even Bobby Thompson's house and my house on Toronto Avenue. There is a great crater and dark pitch-black-like tar smoldering in the ruin of my childhood. Burning still are the houses I once know, raging in inferno they that streets no more where we played and had lives of wonder once. Parkside Field turned to dust, the high school goal posts still glowing red in the darkened night, the night of death and over with glowing red it symbolizes the town, the hero once, the football scores, the glowing red crossbars still standing are all that's left of Massapequa the school the bricks the town the postman the doctors and the teachers too. All dust and the woods so lovely dark and deep with birds and feathers and lovely leaves of spring and streams all rustling turned to ash, evaporated and burned from the great pine trees the pine cones and the crows, disintegrated destroyed forever, and my backyard on the great screen of death tonight I see sucked like a vacuum in time rotated and twisted deep into the earth. An early photograph of my youth all singed too and burned at the edges, a photograph on fire, everything gone, everything precious and dear and lost and lonely—nothing more not even a leaf a pine needle or a squirrel. Nothing to be angry about any more, nothing, not a thing to feel again not a thing to be but blackened landscape, frozen.

I closed my eyes, and still the horrifying nightmare continued. I slept and still it pursued me, ranting and raving. My mother, my father, my sisters, my brothers, the town, all of them everywhere. Oh, Christ, oh, God.

"To be or not to be," shouted the Chief.

"To be," said the Doctor. "To be never and ever what not want hate that got what nots tots nots tots," said the Doctor with a short little giggle as he twisted once again before me on the floor.

"You're all right?" I shouted. "Doctor Twist, Carmen, Richie, Chief? You're all OK?"

"Shan't I can't I will I won't I did I do die dum dee day say why. Not why," said Richie.

"Say when," said the Doctor.

"Say now, never," said the Chief.

"What are you talking about? What do you mean," I shouted.

"Say six-shooters and guns," said the Chief.

"Say wide-angle lenses and sniper scopes and Easter bunnies," said Richie.

"Manifest Destiny!" said the Chief.

"Fifty-four-forty or fight," cried Richie.

"What's yours is mine," said the Doctor.

"VIETNAM!" I screamed.

"Bamboo!" screamed the Chief.

"Hot!" said Carmen.

"Bamboo!" said the Doctor sharply.

"Bamboo!" said Richie.

"A shortcut," said the Doctor.

"I'm hurt," I shouted.

"Just closer," said the Doctor.

82

"Booby traps," said Richie.

"Ambushes," said the Chief.

"In December," I cried.

"By the river," said Carmen.

"On a Tuesday," said the Doctor.

"With barrels blazing," I shouted.

"In the wigwams," shouted the Chief.

"I'm hurt."

"You're close," said the Chief.

"Carmen," I screamed. "Carmen, please touch me."

"In December" whispered Carmen, reaching for my hand.

"In the wigwam," I said.

"No, in the ditch," said the Doctor.

"With guns blazing," said Richie.

"With children and old men crying," said Carmen.

"Along the river" said the Doctor.

"With blood flowing!" I cried. "With blood everywhere!"

"On a Tuesday," said Carmen.

"In the wigwam," said the Doctor.

"They resisted!" I screamed.

"By the river," said the Chief.

"Vietnam!" I cried.

"Bamboo!" screamed the Chief.

"Too late," said the Doctor.

"How did it ever happen?" asked the Chief.

"How did it happen?" said the Doctor.

"Tell us how it happened," said Carmen.

"Yes, tell us," said Richie.

"I used to watch them killing people on television—cowboys killing Indians. I didn't know what killing really meant until I killed that night. I had never killed before I pulled the trigger of my rifle, and in a moment they were dead. I wonder if they heard the cracks, exploding like firecrackers next to their faces on that December night. What do you say to someone you've killed? How do you go about talking to someone who's dead? 'Below, there you lie in your grave because of me'?" I pointed to the floor where suddenly there appeared a simple granite stone.

"'What did you think in the hut that night we killed you? Did you have any idea what was about to happen? Were you awake? Were you asleep? Were you cooking your dinner over a stove? It was evening. You had made a fire the way you did every night. There were pots and pans, the evening meal scattered among your bodies wounded and bleeding. The night we shot you was cold. It was December, a Tuesday, and it had been raining. You were probably getting ready to sit down for dinner, the old man, the father and his three children, the way we used to do in Massapequa with mom and dad and my brothers and sisters.'

"They were talking about something that night the way they did every night at dinnertime, the way everybody talks after their father has come home from work, and he'd been fishing all day long out in the sea near the mouth of the river Cua Viet. They were hungry, and we were moving toward them. There was the lieutenant, and me and the others. They were eating rice and laughing. Slowly in the rain we came looking for the enemy, with rifles in our hands. The old man had made a good catch that day. It was going to be a good week.

84

"We were cold and tired and frustrated. The major wasn't happy. We weren't killing enough VC. We weren't being aggressive enough. The little boy was looking at his grandfather, an old man with a long white beard. He had seen many springs come and go at the mouth of the river Cua Viet. Life will continue, the little boy's grandfather says with his eyes. I have seen many soldiers from different lands come here to the mouth of this river, and each one that has come has gone, and they will come again and go again but they will never stay because this land is not theirs. It is ours. They have not fished in the river and the sea, and they have not worked in our fields with the water buffalo. They only destroy. They are blind men with blind dreams. The old man knew. He had seen many springs, many soldiers.

"Their meal was interrupted, their quiet moment of peace together. Men in uniforms with guns one hundred meters in front of their home.

"December 1967. On a Tuesday. We were lining up behind a rice dike in the rain. We pointed our rifles directly at the hut with the flickering light. We could smell the smoke from their dinner, strange and distant like the land. They did not know we were there. They continued to eat and laugh and talk and enjoy their family together despite the war. We were angry and tired. We wanted VC. We were cold and shivering in the night. We opened fire. We fired again and again, one hundred bullets cracking into their home at once. The men cursed and screamed, the roar of their weapons cracking and exploding. The shock of that moment. The old man leaning over to pour some tea.

85

The three small children eating their soup. The father contemplating the day. The shock of it. Their whole world suddenly and violently exploding all around them in a hail of terror and fire dead and bleeding blood and screams, moaning and death cries, 'My God! My God! What's happened? What hit us?'

"'A mistake. We thought you were the enemy. You were just a bunch of civilians. Sorry, we won't do it again. We'll try not to do it again.' The men falling to their knees, dropping their rifles. I remember that night. Yes, December on a Tuesday. Their cries their screams. The old man with the top of his head blown off, his brains dangling out like jelly. The children scattered all over the hut shot through their stomachs through arms and legs, children crying and screaming, pools and rivers of blood and the rain kept pouring down harder and harder. They kept screaming and the fire had been blown out by the blast of our rifles and they kept screaming and screaming and I could smell their blood and I knelt down and there was blood everywhere soaking through their clothing and the father was screaming something in Vietnamese. He was cursing at me and waving his wounded arm crazily in the air. He kept cursing and I screamed for the men to help.

"'Help them! Help them!' I cried. 'Help the wounded! We made a mistake. We shot the wrong people. We made a fucking mistake.'

"I grabbed for my medical bag and there was blood everywhere. I tried to help. They kept screaming. The blood was cold on my hands and it was raining and I went to bandage the little boy's foot and as I reached for it, it fell off. On a Tuesday. He was screaming and his sister was shot in the stomach and bleeding out of her rear end. The choppers came. Everybody was crying now. They were saying Jesus please forgive us Mary mother of God forgive us. It was December and it was raining and the blood covered my hands and it felt cold. I bandaged the little boy's foot back on to his leg. 'It'll be all right,' I told him. 'Don't worry, it'll be OK.' And I cried and the choppers came and they took them away and I can never forget that night. I can still see their faces and hear their screams. It was December in the rain, and we thought they were the enemy. We made a mistake. We didn't know."

I began to cry. Carmen gently touched my hand.

"A month later I got shot. I was leading my squad across an open area, attacking a village. There was a burning sensation. It was wet, wet like the children had been wet the night of the ambush. I fell to my knees, the bullets still cracking all around me. I reached down with my hand into my pants. My penis was shot off. The bullet had cut my penis off. The bullets were still cracking, and blood was spurting everywhere, I stuffed my fist where my penis used to be, trying to stop the bleeding and I felt dizzy and sick and I was frightened to death and I just wanted to get out of there and live. I didn't care about anything, just getting out of there and staying alive. I never dreamed it would happen this way. I never thought it would happen to me. 'My penis! My penis!' I screamed. 'Somebody shot off my fucking penis!' And they came and got me, and they dragged me back.

"And that's the last thing I remember.

"They sent me home, and I had nightmares all the time. I kept dreaming that I was back in Vietnam, back at the mouth of the river Cua Viet with the bunkers and the rain and the hootches and the heat and the men walking past me in the sand in their jungle boots with their rifles in their hands and fear on their faces. It was a recurring nightmare that repeated itself again and again. I couldn't understand why I was back in the war when I was supposed to be home and the war was supposed to be over with for me. I was afraid, and I kept trying to find a phone so I could call my father back in Massapequa. Maybe my dad can help get me out of here. I've got to get back home. Somebody made a mistake. Can you help me dad? I'm trapped here in Vietnam, and I can't get out of here. It's dangerous here, dad. There's artillery attacks and people getting killed all the time, and ambushes and children screaming in the night. You got to get me out of here dad. I want to come back home to Massapequa, back home to you and mom and the way it was when I was a boy and the war hadn't happened yet, when things were peaceful and I still had my penis and it was safe and I didn't have to be so afraid. When can I come home dad? When is it going to end?

"But my father would not listen."

My whole body was shaking now, and I could no longer speak. I kept crying and Carmen touched my face, then kissed me.

"It hurts," I cried. "Even after all these years it still hurts very much."

The Doctor, Richie and the Chief walked over to

where I was standing and touched me with their hands, not saying anything for a long time.

"On a Tuesday," I said. "In raincoats," I cried. "Bamboo," whispered the Chief. "Bamboo".

I awoke to a day and a morning brighter and more hopeful than any I had felt before in my life. Above me was a reflecting pool and then a light far in the distance that shone through a crack in a ceiling that I could crawl through. Upon entering the other side I could see Massapequa and Bobby Thompson far in the distance. I now ran with everything that was left in me. I had to tell them what I had seen. I had to warn them, wake them up before it was too late. I was exhausted. I could hardly go any further, but I kept running and running towards my town, and as I came closer I could see that the town I had grown up in as a boy had changed. It was different. There was something about it that would never be the same again.

"Bobby! Bobby!" I cried as I reached the front stoop of his house. "It's so good to see you, Bobby. It's so good to be home again."

But Bobby did not see me. He just looked away, above me and through me as if I did not exist.

"Bobby! Don't you remember me? I'm your friend, the guy who made a bet with you." I ran into his house. His father was sleeping on the couch and above his head was a calendar.

"Mr. Thompson, Mr. Thompson!" I shouted, but he would not wake up. I tried to shake him, but I could not touch him. I couldn't reach him or feel him. All I felt was myself, standing there.

"I'm not going on any more dumb trips!" I shouted to Bobby's father. "I've had enough of all this crazy traveling for a while. I'm just going to stay here in Massapequa and maybe get a haircut." I walked out of the house.

"I'm through with both of you," I shouted. "I don't want your money," I said to Bobby as I started walking across his front lawn. "You can have your stupid life savings," I said. "I'm going home."

CITY LIGHTS PUBLICATIONS

Pickard, Tom. *GUTTERSNIPE*
Plymell, Charles. *THE LAST OF THE MOCCASINS*
Poe, Edgar Allan. *THE UNKNOWN POE*
Prévert, Jacques. *PAROLES (Pocket Poets #9)*
Rips, Geoffrey. *UNAMERICAN ACTIVITIES*
Rosemont, Franklin. *SURREALISM & ITS
      POPULAR ACCOMPLICES*
Sanders, Ed. *INVESTIGATIVE POETRY*
Shepard, Sam. *FOOL FOR LOVE*
Shepard, Sam. *MOTEL CHRONICLES*
Snyder, Gary. *THE OLD WAYS*
Solomon, Carl. *MISHAPS PERHAPS*
Solomon, Carl. *MORE MISHAPS*
Svevo, Italo. *JAMES JOYCE*
Upton, Charles. *PANIC GRASS (Pocket Poets #24)*
Voznesensky, Andrei. *DOGALYPSE (Pocket Poets #29)*
Waldman, Anne. *FAST SPEAKING WOMAN (Pocket Poets #33)*
Waley, Arthur. *THE NINE SONGS*
Yevtushenko, Yevgeni. *RED CATS (Pocket Poets #16)*